A BETTER LOSER

Nathan Graziano

ROADSIDE PRESS

Editor: Michele McDannold

Roadside Press
Colchester, Illinois

Table of Contents

Part III

For Liz, for always

"Should I, after tea and cakes and ices,
  Have the strength to force the moment to its crisis?"
—T.S. Eliot, "The Love Song of J. Alfred Prufrock"

"Once I was strong but I lost the fight.
  You won't find a better loser."
—Derek and the Dominoes, "Bell Bottom Blues"

Part I

VANDALS

THE FIRST SUGGESTION WAS toilet paper. Then, as I watched a gapped grin spread across Geoff's face, I knew that eggs would be involved, too.

Larry's house was going down.

It was Halloween in 1987, and I was twelve years old. The day before, my parents sat down my sister and me at the kitchen table to give us the speech—not to be confused with "The Speech," that infinitely awkward birds and bees business. I never got that one from either of my parents. I learned about sex by flipping through a stack of *Hustler* that Geoff's older brother, Paul, hid in his bedroom closet. After walking in and finding us with his magazines fanned out on the floor one day, Paul gave us his boiled-down-to-the-essentials version of "The Speech." It went like this: "If your dick is pointing up, put a rubber on it."

Instead, my parents were about to give us the other speech that no kid wants to hear. Mom sat across from Anna and me with her hands folded on the table, while my father paced back and forth behind her with his head down, puffing on a Marlboro while palming a can of Budweiser.

Mom said, "We want you both to know that we love you very much, and this is in no way your fault." The muscles in her face tightened as she patted her eyes with a tissue.

I had been expecting this. A couple of weeks before, while my mom was working the second shift at the hospital, I overheard my father on the telephone in their bedroom, telling the person on the other line that he was planning to leave Mom. However, my sister Anna, who was two years younger than me, didn't suspect a thing, and as soon as my mother told us that they were getting a divorce, Anna leaped up from her chair, crying and covering her face with her hands, then bolted to her bedroom.

Then my parents started getting into it.

"That went well. Good plan, Julia," my father said as he cracked open another can of beer.

"Why do you always have to be such a fucking asshole, Don?"

"Our son is right here."

"He should know it, too." Mom turned to me. "Your father is a fucking asshole!"

I had enough and got up and told them I was going to Geoff's house. Geoff's mother, who divorced his dad when Geoff was too young to remember, worked two jobs and was hardly ever home. At first, Mom didn't want me going over there when his mother wasn't around, claiming she heard rumors that Geoff's older brother smoked pot, which he did.

Now, with dark bags beneath her eyes and the skin on her face pale and drawn, Mom was tired of fighting—tired of fighting with me, tired of fighting with my father—and when I said I was going to Geoff's house, she relented with a flick of her wrist.

My father didn't say a word. He didn't even look at me when I said I was leaving. He drank his beer and seethed in silence.

While Halloween was already ruined for me, Geoff and I still planned to dress the trees in our neighbor's front yard with toilet paper and pelt his house with eggs.

By 3 p.m. on Halloween, we were sitting cross-legged on the floor in Geoff's bedroom, surrounded by posters of our New England sports heroes: Roger Clemens on the pitcher's mound, mid-delivery, his head turning toward home plate; Larry Bird lining up a jumper; and Andre Tippett about to level a crushing blow on a halfback. Geoff reached under his bed and pulled out two rolls of toilet paper and a carton of eggs that he had lifted from his fridge.

"I have something else," he said, again reaching under the bed for a shoebox filled with baseball cards, the entire 1986 Topps collection. He removed something from the shoebox and closed his hand around it. "Guess what it is."

"Your mom's panties?" I said, standing up. "Let's listen to Bon Jovi."

"Paul says all of the guys in Bon Jovi are homos. He says Jon Bon Jovi has AIDS, and we should listen to Metallica instead."

Shrugging, I rewound the cassette of *Slippery When Wet* in Geoff's deck to listen to "Livin' on a Prayer." I liked the voice box at the beginning, and the couple in the song, staying together through all of those hard times, reminded me of my parents—when they used to get along, that is. Like the guy in the song, my father once played the guitar in a band then he had to pawn his Stratocaster after he got married and his band broke up. That's when he started getting drunk every night.

"What's in your hand?" I asked Geoff.

Geoff held out his fist, unfurling one finger at a time. In his palm laid something that looked like a shriveled cigarette. "I stole it from Paul."

"What is it?"

"It's a joint, you retard. It's supposed to make you go psycho," he said. "I figured we'd smoke it before we hit Larry's house tonight."

My jaw dropped like it was attached by wires that Geoff just sliced. When I pledged to become a member of Nancy Reagan's D.A.R.E. program, I had signed a contract stating I'd

"Just Say No" if someone offered drugs to me. I'd seen the commercial with the fried egg—this is your brain on drugs—a million times. Drugs were bad, potentially deadly.

But there was another part of me that liked the idea of being bad. Little was I aware that this part of me would eventually seize control of my life, like it did with my father, and, eventually, this part of me would cost me my marriage and turn me into a fucking asshole, like my father.

Someone knocked on the bedroom door, and Geoff's eyes widened. Terrified his mother had come home early from work, he tossed the joint under his bed.

"Open the door, shit stain."

Geoff unlocked the door, and Paul strolled in, his thumbs hitched in the belt loops of his nut-hugger acid-washed jeans. He wore a faded Iron Maiden t-shirt and his dirty-blond hair was feathered in the front and fell to his shoulders in the back. Immediately, he went to the boom box and shut off the music.

"Bon Jovi's a faggot," he said. "Listen dildos, Debbie's coming over, and if either of you interrupt us, I'll rip off your arms and beat you with them." He looked at me. "Hey Mark, does what's-her-name still babysit for you?"

"Danielle," I said, although Paul knew her name and once shared with us a rather thorough list of things he would like to do, sexually, to her face. "She says you're a druggie."

"She's a slut," Paul said, running a black comb that surfaced from his back pocket through his hair. "She's got some big tits, though. I'd like to bury my face between those puppies and motorboat the shit out of those titties."

I glanced at Geoff. While I had looked at the breasts on the girls in *Hustler*, the appeal was not exactly sexual—not yet. The thrill, instead, lay in seeing what I was not meant to see, what was forbidden and hidden from me. But that would soon change. Within two years, I'd be willing to crawl on my stomach through broken glass to get my hands on a set of breasts.

Paul flipped us the double-birds, grabbed his balls, and made for the door. "Catch you later, faggots."

As soon as Paul left, Geoff was, again, holding the joint and letting it roll in his cupped hand. "This won't make us act like him, will it?"

My father didn't come home for dinner on Halloween night. This was the first time my father skipped dinner when my mother wasn't working, the first of many dinners missed, until he would finally move out of the house and in with his girlfriend after Christmas.

Mom tried to be nonchalant by humming "Bridge over Troubled Water" while we waited for him to come home. After twenty minutes, with the pork chops and potatoes and green beans warming in the oven, she resigned herself to the fact that he wouldn't be home and told Anna and me to grab our plates. Deep down, I think Mom still wanted the marriage to work, despite the fact that she probably knew my father was cheating on her. For the first six months after he moved out, I would hear Mom on the phone at night with one of her sisters, crying and spitting my father's name like it was poison.

My father, on the other hand, was dating our babysitter's mother, who would later become my stepmother, and he never mentioned Mom's name, unless Anna or I brought her up. Danielle also stopped babysitting for us soon after my father stopped showing up for dinner.

At first, no one spoke at the kitchen table. Our silverware scraping against the plates only amplified the silence. Mom tried smiling, but her eyes, glossed-over and focused on the wall clock, weren't into it. Then she tried to engage us in conversation.

"What are you going to dress as tonight, Mark?"

"I'm borrowing an Alf mask from Geoff," I said without looking up from my plate.

"Are you going trick-or-treating, or are you too old for that?" While not oblivious to it, my mother found my approaching adolescence unsettling, bothersome, like a dull ache that was difficult to locate.

I continued to stare at my plate. "Maybe," I mumbled, careful to conceal my real plans. I'm still not entirely sure why we were so hell-bent on hitting Larry's house, or why we had to get high to do it. The ostensible reason, I guess, was that Larry—a beer-bellied man in his mid-thirties with a thick bushy beard and narrow eyes—was an asshole. He was obsessed with his lawn and ornery about it, sometimes threatening to have the neighborhood kids who trespassed on it arrested. But this didn't stop me from cutting through his yard to get to Geoff's house. A couple of times, Larry caught me on his lawn and came to his door and screamed that he was calling the cops as I sprinted away. Larry and his wife were one of the few couples in our neighborhood on the north end of Manchester without kids of their own, so when it came to dealing with other people's children, especially when it came to the boys, Larry was a notorious dick. Rumors had circulated that he once pulled a shotgun on Mike Hague, whose family moved to Hawaii when I was in the second grade, but no one could confirm the story, and it was likely just an urban legend. Regardless, as Geoff and I were making our plans to hit Larry's house that Halloween, the shotgun lingered like a phantom limb.

"What about you, Anna?" Mom asked and smiled at my sister sitting across from me at the dinner table. "Are you going out with your friends tonight?"

"You said you were going to take me trick-or-treating," Anna said.

"I did?" My mom slapped her hand against her forehead. "That's right. I did." Her head jerked back like she'd been grabbed by the hair and snapped forward into her hands. Then our mom—the unshakeable foundation of our family, the woman who made our meals and checked our homework and attended to our every need—was bawling into her small, thin hands.

Stunned and confused, I stood up and rubbed Mom's back as Anna draped her arms around Mom's neck. The weeping continued for what seemed like hours but, in actuality, it was no longer than a minute.

Finally, Mom lifted her head and wiped her eyes with the heels of her hands. "That fucking asshole," she said, sniffling. Then she looked at me. "Don't grow up to be a fucking asshole like your father."

"I won't," I said.

Lo and behold, I did.

Pell Elementary School was within walking distance of our houses, so when Geoff and I needed a spot to smoke the joint, we decided to go to the playground, which we knew would be dark and empty. We sat side by side on the swings with our feet dangling off the ground, trying to decide which end of the joint to light.

"Light the end without the filter," I said, the Alf mask—with its large latex snout and faux orange fur—rested in my lap.

"Joints don't have filters, you dumb shit." Geoff was dressed as a deranged hobo, wearing a faded pair of his uncle's dress pants and red suspenders. With his mother's black eyeliner, he penciled in a scruffy beard on his freckled skin then dabbed some fake blood on his forehead. He carried a toy shotgun that, he claimed, made him "deranged." When he flicked the lighter, his bald face glowed in the flame's light and, for a moment, I could see what Geoff would look like as an adult. "I guess it doesn't matter which end I light," he said.

He placed the joint between his lips and slowly, like a lazy sunrise, lifted the flame to the end of it. The paper caught, and Geoff made a slurping noise like he was sucking through a straw. He held his breath as the smoke funneled from his nostrils and lips like an engine overheating, and then he coughed a tremendous cloud, hacking for a good minute before handing me the joint.

"I can feel it already," he said. "I think I'm stoned."

"You're full of shit."

"I swear to God. I feel thick. My skin is really thick."

When I went to take a hit of the joint, it had gone out, so I had to relight it and ended up torching half the thing in the process. The paper burned unevenly, which I had never seen happen with my father's cigarettes, and I took a tiny hit, not giving the smoke the opportunity to fill my mouth before I was blowing it out, coughing and gagging. We went back and forth like this a couple of times, trying to seem casual and comfortable in our new roles as potheads.

A pair of headlights lit up the slide to our left as I was holding the joint. Spooked, I dropped it and ran with Geoff into the woods behind the playground. Hidden by the trees, we watched as a black Camaro parked in a teacher's spot in the lot outside the playground and switched off the headlights. With the engine running, the passenger door opened as Whitesnake's "Here We Go Again" blasted from the car stereo. A girl got out.

"I'll be right back," the girl said and closed the car door. I recognized the voice. It was Danielle, my babysitter, and although neither of us knew it yet, in less than a year, she would become my stepsister.

The driver's window rolled down. "Do you want me to spark one?" called a male voice from inside the car. "You like to fuck when you're high, right?"

Danielle giggled. "I like to fuck when I'm not."

She approached the woods, humming something tuneless as her footsteps grew louder, like she was a character in a horror film, unaware of the madman lurking in the darkness. Frozen by fear, Geoff and I held our breath. I put on my Alf mask, just in case.

A few feet into the woods, Danielle stopped and unbuckled her jeans, standing in front of the tree Geoff was hiding behind. From the corner of my eye, I watched as she pulled down her panties and squatted. Listening to her urinate thrilled me more than the naked women in the magazines. And by the time Danielle stood up straight and zipped up, I had an erection that I didn't understand. I didn't feel high, just dirty and guilty.

As she was walking back to the car, Danielle stopped at the swings, bent down, and picked up the joint that I dropped and sniffed it. "Hey Casey, you're never going to guess what I found."

We waited until the car left the lot then Geoff looked at me and cocked his head in the direction of our neighborhood. "Let's get out of here," he whispered, and we booked it back to the neighborhood with Larry's house lingering in our crosshairs.

"You don't feel anything? Not even lightheaded?" Geoff asked.

"I don't feel anything," I said, taking off the Alf mask. The chilled night air felt good against my skin. The streets were mostly empty by this time, the porch lights on most of the houses had been turned off. The final October moon was almost full, with the exception of a nibble bitten off its corner, and the streetlights held our shadows, giant versions of ourselves on the concrete. I wanted to go home, but Geoff talked me into hitting Larry's house first. We decided not to toilet-paper the tree in front. It was too dangerous, and both of us were tired.

"I'm definitely feeling something," Geoff said, "but I'm not sure what it is. I think I'm high."

"I don't know," I said, conceding to a bit of lightheadedness. "Maybe I am, too."

We turned onto Larry's street, which had a cul-de-sac at the end and more woods beyond it. "What time do you have to be home?" Geoff asked.

I flipped on my mask. "My mom didn't say." And she hadn't. She had barely noticed me leave. "My parents are getting divorced," I said. It was the first time I said it aloud, and the words tumbled off my tongue like tiny stones.

"That sucks." Geoff held a pillowcase with the toilet paper and eggs in one hand and the toy shotgun in the other. "It seems like my parents have always hated each other," he said. Then Geoff grabbed me by the arm. "Stop. Get down."

We crouched behind a gray hatchback parked in front of Larry's house. The house lights were off, except for a window in the basement where the bluish glow of a television set shimmered in the frame. Maybe Larry was watching a show with his wife, a rope thin woman named Fran. His wife usually worked the graveyard shift at the same hospital as my mom, so people rarely saw Fran. The shade in one window, which I assume was their bedroom, was always pulled down during the daytime. Mom went to high school with Fran, and I remember Mom telling my father at dinner one night how she would occasionally run into her at the hospital. She told him that Fran and Larry were "still trying," which meant nothing to me at the time. If I'd understood it then, I like to think that I wouldn't have done what I was about to do. But that's probably not true.

Geoff reached in the pillowcase and handed me an egg. "After we throw them, run."

With the egg in the palm of my hand, I closed my fingers around it, and the egg seemed to disappear. My father would always brag about the wild things he did with his friends when he was younger. One time, he got arrested for getting drunk and streaking through the police station, and another time, one Halloween when he was in high school, my father and his buddies stole a bunch of pumpkins from other people's front steps and put them on the principal's lawn. And until the day he died of lung cancer, my dad liked to talk about playing with his band and going out to gigs and raising hell. Then, he'd tell us, he got married and had kids and nothing was ever fun again, he'd say, shaking his head while sipping a beer.

I wound up and threw the egg at the house. It hit the front siding beside the door. Geoff threw his egg and hit a window. The porch light switched on, and Geoff and I turned and sprinted down the street, running until we hit the woods where we stopped to catch our breath.

Geoff said, "That was awesome."

"Do you have any more eggs?"

"Almost a whole carton."

"Let's do it again."

"Do you feel high yet?"

"I'm definitely feeling something."

MINOR KEYS

I WAS STONED, TOO STONED, and I began to worry that I would forget how to breathe. That's when Mike jammed another joint in my face. "Have another hit, baby," he said.

I pushed it away.

"Then I have something else you can put your lips on," Mike whispered in my ear, nuzzling my neck with his scruff.

"Stop," I said in a voice so tiny it could've come from a doll. When Mike wanted me to do something, I seldom raised a fuss, mostly because he was ten years older than me and a former-Marine and muscular enough to pose for the cover of a fitness magazine. My best friend Erin told me that I was seeking a father-figure, seeing I barely knew my real dad, a deadbeat who never bothered to get involved in my life.

Mike's roommate Jayce was sitting across the room, staring at me without blinking. With his shaved head and neck tattoos, Jayce was a real creep. I'd only met him a few times and he never said much. He would just stare at my chest in the same way some of the pervs who taught at my high school would stare at me during class, like they were hungry. Jayce was recently released from county jail after serving six months, but Mike didn't tell me what he was in for, and I didn't ask. Jayce kept staring at me, making me more paranoid and giving me the chills.

Mike finally caught on. "Don't you be staring at my girl, bro," Mike said.

"My bad," said Jayce in a flat voice and kept staring.

I focused on a crack in the plaster on the living room wall, mostly to keep the room from spinning. The apartment was on the first floor of an old house in downtown Manchester, and there was a heroin trap house across the street with junkies always running in and out. The walls were all cracked, and the worn blue carpet reminded me of a sick old woman. At that moment, more than anything, I wanted to be in my bed, under the covers, watching videos on YouTube and not listening to the rap music that Mike was blasting through a Bluetooth speaker.

I glanced at my phone and had texts from Erin and my mother. I opened the text from my mom first. It read: *Where are u? I'm worried. Call me, plz.* Mom was on her third round of chemo and always at home and constantly worried about me.

Mike then placed his hand, a vise grip, on my thigh and squeezed it hard enough to leave finger marks. "Have another White Claw," he said over the music and handed me a can. Then he stood up and went into the kitchen to do another line of coke. He tried to get me to try it, but I don't really like drugs, and the weed had already messed me up.

As soon as Mike left the room, I started to reply to Mom, to make up a lie about where I was, but Jayce's stare smothered me, like his eyes were heat lamps. This time, he cocked his head to the side and tried looking up my skirt. "You're fucking hot," he yelled over the music.

I swallowed a sip of the hard seltzer and smiled crookedly, scared. When Mike came back, sniffing, he sat beside me and placed his hand back on my thigh, snaking it up my skirt. I tried to move it.

I dropped my phone between the cushions and sprung from the couch. "Not with your roommate here," I said.

Mike sighed. "You should probably go home if you don't feel like partying."

"I want to party," I lied. "Let's go in your room," I whispered to Mike.

"Let's do a tequila shot first."

For the second time, Mike left the room, and for the second time, Jayce tried looking up my skirt. I pressed my knees tightly together and reached between the cushions for my phone but couldn't find it.

Mike came back, sniffing, with three shot glasses. He kept one for himself and passed the others to Jayce and me. While Mike and Jayce slammed back the shots, fast and smooth, I plugged my nose like I was about to dive into dirty water and poured it down my throat, coughing and gagging as the tequila dropped like a hot knife in my belly. Mike leaned over and licked my neck. "You're so fucking hot."

"Let's go to your room."

"I have a better idea. Why don't we make a movie and let Jayce record it. I want you to see how sexy you look when we fuck."

I turned my head from Mike's hot breath. The pot and the alcohol and pulsing music and the terror had messed with my sense of balance, turning my legs into noodles. "I feel weird," I said.

"You're fine, baby," Mike said.

I felt myself slipping out of my skin, suddenly very dizzy. The last things I remember were my joints turning to liquid and my head dropping on Mike's lap, my blonde hair landing like a parachute.

"Start the recording," I remember Mike saying as he unzipped his fly, and I blacked out.

The tail lights on Mike's truck grew softer, and then softer, and then disappeared down the dark road. My mom and my stepfather didn't care for Mike, so I didn't want to be dropped off at home after I regained consciousness and needed to sleep in my own bed. Instead, I had him leave me about a quarter of a mile down the road, in front of a white ranch with the porch lights still on. Dusk had started to break, the horizon turning a soft orange. I fell to my hands and knees on the damp grass and started to heave.

Meanwhile, down the road, a bald woman wearing a lavender headscarf with her eyebrows penciled in was probably pacing the kitchen floor, stopping in front of the sink and pouring herself a glass of tap water to wash down the pain pills. I knew my mother wouldn't *really* sleep until I walked through that door, and I was disoriented and had somehow left my phone at Mike's apartment so I couldn't call.

With my hair covering my face, I spit bile on the grass that was slick with morning dew. I wished I would pass out and lose consciousness again, anything to stop the sickness; anything to stop the hazy images flashing through my head of Mike grabbing me by my hair and shoving himself into my mouth until I gagged and vomited, and his roommate recording it with his phone in one hand and stroking himself with the other before the curtain dropped on my memories; anything to get back what I left at that apartment.

Anything to make it stop.

I fell to my stomach, my cheek pressed to the cold ground, and wept as my eyes closed and I passed out again.

The sunlight stung my eyes as they opened. Somehow, the owners of the house, a Candia cop and his wife, hadn't noticed me on the side of it. Wanting nothing more than a hot shower, I brushed off my legs and started up the road until I reached our dirt driveway and turned toward the house.

My stepfather Wayne and his two best friends who played in a rock band with him were sitting on lawn chairs under an awning outside Wayne's RV, the cooler iced and packed with beer first thing in the morning. It was their Saturday routine until the winter came and forced them indoors. On Friday nights, they would play their weekly gig at a local bar called Glory Jeans, the other guys often sleeping in the camper, and then on Saturday mornings, they got up and drank all day, usually having friends hang out around the fire pit once it got dark.

An enormous man, Wayne stood up when he saw me at the end of the driveway and waved. "Darla, she's home," he yelled.

I kept my head down, biting my bottom lip as I tried to walk past Wayne without stopping. But he stepped in front of me and lifted my chin with his index finger. "What the hell happened to you, Jenny?"

"Nothing really," I said and hurried past him and in the side door.

My mother was sitting at the kitchen table in her ratty pink bathrobe, a hideous wig of straight black hair crooked on her head. "Where the hell were you? I tried calling you all night, and there was no answer. I was about to call the police. I thought you were dead." Then when she saw me, *really* saw me, she clasped her chest. "My God. My baby."

I moved to the sink and poured a glass of water as Mom rose from her chair with her mouth open and arms outstretched, her words stuck like a nail in her throat. Then, in what seemed like slow motion, she collapsed.

"Mom!"

When she hit the ground, the wig fell off—her scalp exposed. I remember screaming, falling to my knees and cradling her bald head in my arms. I pleaded with her not to die. Not now. Not yet.

And she didn't die. Not then. Not yet.

■■■

Wayne rolled down the driver's side window and lit a cigarette. It was almost 1 a.m., and I sat beside him in his truck on the way back from the hospital. After seeing Mom, so pale and weak, lying in that hospital bed with that stupid wig on her head, I had temporarily vacuumed up the pain and humiliation from the other night, placing it on a shelf in my mind. However, like the IV drip jammed into my mother's forearm, the pain and humiliation was slowly returning in drops, drop by drop.

At the hospital, Mom told Wayne and me the same thing she'd been telling her doctors. "Don't count me out," she said. "I haven't given up." But the facts were the facts: the cancer had metastasized to her bones and liver, and at what point do you stop fighting the things that are inevitable and let life have its way with you? Maybe my mother was showing courage, a courage she wanted me to see, but somehow it seemed pointless.

There wasn't much else to say.

Wayne drove home on a dark back road instead of the highway, the gravel crunching beneath the tires and the radio turned low. "You know, she wants us to keep living together," Wayne said. "Even after."

His bearded profile, the plump cheeks and the thick padding of flesh below his chin, made him look safe, honest and kind. For a man, that is. I almost told him what happened to me, although I wasn't sure what I had to tell. At the time, I suppose I knew what to call it, but I didn't want to use the word. While I wasn't ready to use the word, I realized that what Mike and Jayce did to me was not normal, or kind, or legal. If I told Wayne, he would make me tell the police what had happened, but I couldn't remember anything, and it would be my word against theirs. And did I really want to know what they did to me while I was blacked out? Did I really want to know what Mike had slipped into one of my drinks? A sickness kept churning in my stomach when I thought about the word, like my body needed to purge it. But once I spoke it, I would become a victim. My bottom lip began to tremble and pressure gathered behind my eyes and forehead. I pressed my face against Wayne's shoulder as sobs, not words, exploded from my chest.

Wayne pulled the truck to the side of the road and put his thick arm around me. "It's going to be all right, sweetie."

"It's not fair. It's not right. I don't deserve this."

"I know, sweetheart. No one deserves this, especially your mom."

We stayed on the side of the road for the better part of an hour, saying nothing, as I emptied myself of the pressure behind my eyes. Not a single car, not a single set of headlights passed us. It was almost as if we weren't there.

It rained the next day, and I didn't bother getting out of bed until nightfall. I still didn't have my phone, but I didn't want to go back there to get it. Ever. So I slept and cried and watched YouTube videos on my laptop. By the time I got up, the sky was a clear black pool sprinkled with stars, and the September air had turned cool. While sitting on a stool outside the RV, with wooden Tiki torches driven into the dirt around him, Wayne strummed a slow song on his guitar, a song that sounded a little like a clear night after a rainy day.

Wayne continued to play, acknowledging me with a nod. I sat down in a lawn chair across from him. I watched him, hugging myself. Wayne finished his song and put down the guitar then lit a cigarette. "How are you holding up, kiddo?"

I shrugged. "Not so good."

"Me neither."

"What was that song you were playing?"

"It's nothing yet. I was just messing around with a minor

chord progession. I'm not sure what I'll call it, if I call it anything. I'm not so good when it comes to writing down words. Words aren't my thing."

"I'm not so good with them, either."

The side door opened and D.J., my stepbrother, hunkered down the steps and sat in another lawn chair. Like Wayne, D.J. was large and extremely hairy, and the kids at school, including some of my friends, teased him relentlessly. They called him Sasquatch and threw food at him during lunch. Sometimes I felt bad, but I never told them to stop.

"Don't the two of you have school tomorrow?" Wayne asked as he opened a red cooler and plunged his hand inside, the ice rumbling.

"I'm not going," I said. "I'm going to visit Mom." I thought about going to the police afterwards and reporting Mike and Jayce, having them arrested for what they did, but I also didn't think anyone would believe me, and I just wanted it all to go away. I would've been happy if they just returned my phone, placed it in the mailbox, and drove out of my life forever.

"That sounds fair enough," Wayne said.

"I'm sorry about Darla," D.J. said to me, staring at his hands.

"Thanks."

Wayne reached into the cooler, and when the rumbling of the ice stopped, Wayne's hand appeared holding two cold cans of beer. He handed a beer to me and one to D.J. "Just don't tell no one," Wayne said then picked up his guitar and started to strum again, stopping to tune a bit.

And I didn't tell anyone, not a word.

THE PROUD FATHER

HIS BOTTOM LIP QUIVERS AS HE RISES before the judge, the jury, and the television cameras. He is your son, your only child, and he recently turned eighteen. In his new navy-blue suit and tie—the navy-blue suit and tie you bought him with the money you and your wife had saved for his first semester at Dartmouth—he reminds you of his six-year-old self, a boy with a high blush and a hairless face.

As you watch him, your chest tightens, your left arm goes numb, and you wonder if forty-six is too young to have a heart attack. Your son is being tried as an adult, and you wish you could trade places with his attorney, the man you can't afford, the man with a wizened white beard and a hand resting on your son's shoulder. You want to be close to your son, to hold him.

Your wife squeezes your hand and whimpers. You want to hold her as well, despite her threats of divorce and the accusations that you failed to raise your son to be a decent man. She used that word: *decent*.

You glance across the aisle at the alleged victim and her family, her father hugging her as she wipes her eyes and waits. You want to believe that she perjured herself. You want to believe that she is trying to save face for the bad decision she made after she left the party that night, drunk, with your son. You want to believe that she consented, and that your son—in a terrible moment of unchecked passion—accidentally bit her breast then apologized, like he testified. You want to believe that you're all decent people, parents and children alike, and that something occurred that night in a bedroom behind a locked door at a teenage house party, something as ambiguous as a Rorschach test, something utterly unknowable and mired in reasonable doubt.

And now, as the head juror stands in front of your son, and your wife's hand is sweating and her breathing is labored, you watch him, your boy. He's the boy you coached in Little League, the second baseman and lead-off hitter on a last-place team; the boy you taught to whistle through an acorn; the boy you taught how to jump a stick shift by pushing it down a hill and punching the clutch; the boy you taught to tie a Windsor Knot, something your father taught you. This is your son, and you know, beneath the banter and the bravado, there is a sensitive kid, someone you've been proud to call your son for eighteen years—an honor roll student and an average athlete, a boy who writes poetry but is too insecure to share it with anyone other than you and your wife and, allegedly, the girl across the aisle. And you know—and this is what startles you from sleep—he won't fare well in prison, being so young and fresh-faced and hardly needing to shave.

You wonder, as you squeeze your wife's hand and ignore the tightening in your chest, if your son did what the girl said he did to her, if the events happened the way the girl, talking through choked sobs, testified. You wonder if your son—and this terrifies you the most—is capable of being so monstrous. You question yourself and your own decency.

"Has the jury reached a decision?" The judge asks, peering over her bifocals.

"We have, Your Honor."

The bailiff takes the slip of paper from the head juror and hands it to the judge, who reads it, stone-faced, and hands it back. Your wife whimpers again. Your son squeezes his eyes shut and bites on his bottom lip to keep it from quivering. For a second, the courtroom is as airless as a catacomb. The head juror clears his throat. The cameras click, all of them pointed at your son.

Your heart beats with your son's heart, and you are back to a Christmas morning, your son smiling, silver wrapping paper wadded around him. Later, as your son played his new video game system, giggling with joy, your wife asked if you wanted to try for another. You made love that night. But after the tests and procedures, the false hopes and expensive attempts at In vitro fertilization, you eventually accepted that you were happy to have one—the proud father of his only son.

As the head juror reads the decision, your son's head drops like the tendons were cut in his neck. When he turns to you and wails, and your wife wails, too, your legs give as you try to stand, and your chest tightens.

THE TROUBADOUR OF THE TRASH GODS

MY FIRST LOVE DUMPED ME in the hallway before a Chemistry final. While I tried to muffle my sobs with a closed fist pressed to my mouth, sitting beneath a wall-sized poster of The Periodic Table—blubbering below Berkelium—Mr. Barrett walked up and down the rows of desks, passing out the exam. I bombed it and nearly failed the class, which would have prevented me from graduating the next week. Instead of drawing compounds, I drew pictures of daggers plunging into Blaine McMullen's scrawny chest.

But I squeaked through the course—I suspect Mr. Barrett cooked the grade book to get me through it—still reeling from a broken heart. Then two days before the graduation ceremony, while hitting on a loosely-rolled joint in the passenger seat of Alan's Sentra, "November Rain" came on the radio, and I completely broke down again, this time in front of Alan. The *Use Your Illusion* albums were released in September that year, and my ex-girlfriend Rosie and I skipped school that day and waited in the parking lot with a half dozen metalheads for Harry's Records to open. I bought both albums on cassette, and then Rosie and I went back to my parents' empty house and had sex on my waterbed while listening to them. Rosie was not a huge Guns N' Roses fan, nor had she ever skipped school before—she was the salutatorian of our senior class—but she risked the consequences for me that day, and I was too self-absorbed to appreciate it.

As I bawled, wiping my nose with a snotty sleeve, Alan tapped along with the song on the steering wheel. He was the drummer for our band The Trash Gods, and he was always keeping time on some kind of surface. When I passed the joint back and looked at him—my eyes swollen and tears streaming down my face—he sighed. "You need to get a grip, dude," Alan said, puffing on the joint. "She's moved on, man. Besides, she's leaving for college in a few months, and when The Trash Gods take off, we're going to have chicks begging for our dicks, dude. Trust me."

"But I love her," I said.

"And what do you think is going to happen when she's at college with all of those rich Ivy League pricks driving around campus in their fancy jeeps that their daddies bought them?"

"We're in love, man."

"Then why did she start dating Blaine McMullen the day after she broke up with you? Man, I'll bet she was hooking up with McMullen before she dumped your ass."

"Fuck you."

The afternoon was cloudless and bright, and the sun burned my eyes as I imagined myself standing on top of a grand piano, playing a sleek Les Paul like Slash in the "November Rain" video. I imagined myself tearing through the solo as Rosie looked up at me from the crowd, her green eyes pleading for me to take her back as she realized the tremendous mistake she'd made that morning in the hallway, tossing me aside for that egg-head.

"Sorry, amigo, but you need to accept the truth," Alan said, running his fingers through his long, wavy blond hair. A short and scrawny guy, Alan's lustrous mane made him seem three inches taller, and his hair was the envy of every girl in our school—nary a split-end. I was also in the process of growing out my mousy brown hair to give The Trash Gods more rock n' roll credentials, but my hair was straight and shaggy, my bangs hanging like ragged drapes over my eyes. The band consisted of me, singing and playing guitar, Alan on the drums, and Corky D'Amato—who had a near-perfect mullet—on the bass. We played two original songs and a dozen covers, ranging from Led Zeppelin and Neil Young to a punked-out version of "Summer of '69." While we had never played a paying gig—although sometimes a hat was passed around at house parties—we were committed to busting out of Corky's parents' basement where we practiced. There was only one small problem: We weren't very good.

As I reached on the dashboard for my plastic sunglasses, I was struck by a sudden inspiration, an idea birthed from my crippling heartbreak. I said to Alan, "I know what I'm going to do."

"What are you going to do, dude?"

I put on the sunglasses and reclined in the passenger seat. "I'm going to write Rosie a love song."

My bedroom was in the basement of my parents' house, one of fifty near-identical raised ranches in a suburb in Hooksett, where every house had hand-painted mailboxes and an American flag hanging beside the front door. My parents' bedroom and my older sister Tricia's empty one were upstairs, so the finished basement—complete with a half-bathroom—functioned like my own private flat. On weekends, Rosie would leave through the front door for her curfew at midnight, park down the street then sneak back in through my bedroom window. She would tell her parents she was sleeping at her friend Amanda's house, and Rosie and I would spend the night together, canoodling on my waterbed and setting the alarm for 6 a.m. so she could scoot out the window and get back home before our parents woke up.

After Alan dropped me off that afternoon, as my weed buzz waned, I sat in my bedroom with the window open, fiddling with some chords on my acoustic guitar as an evening breeze cut through the room. The shouts from kids playing Wiffle ball in a neighbor's backyard echoed in the distance as I strummed an A-minor, waiting for the articulation of my pain to congeal into music, waiting for those words with my notebook open and a pen beside it, waiting for my love song to arrive.

I decided that my creativity could use a jumpstart, so I put down my guitar and went to the sock drawer of my dresser for the cigar box where I had a dime bag and two small roaches. As soon as I fastened a roach to an elaborate clip I had made with an eagle feather, a cowhide string and superglue, someone knocked at my bedroom door. "Just a minute," I said, closing the cigar box and shoving everything back into the sock drawer.

"I hope you're not doing anything you shouldn't be," Mom said.

I opened the bedroom door and rubbed my eyes, still swollen and bloodshot. "I was trying to take a nap," I said.

Mom came in wearing her work clothes—she was a secretary at a middle school in Manchester—and her eyes were also swollen and bloodshot. The blonde dye had faded in the part of her shoulder-length hair, exposing the gray roots. Deep-purple bags dug beneath her eyes. I wasn't supposed to be privy to this information, but I had known since my sophomore year—Tricia told me before she left for the University of Southern Maine— that our parents were planning to separate after I graduated.

Mom rested her thin shoulder against the door frame, a small smile creeping from the corner of her mouth. "Can we talk?" she asked.

"About what?" I plopped down on my waterbed with my arms behind my head, staring at the ceiling.

Mom sat in the desk chair across from me. "I'm worried about you, Pudge."

"Please don't call me that." Right before I hit puberty and my first growth spurt, I was a little butterball in the sixth grade and acquired that ghastly nickname from a baseball coach, ostensibly paying homage to Carlton Fisk. Unfortunately, the nickname stuck. My entire life, since that first growth spurt, I've been battling with my weight, and that nickname still irks me to no end.

"I'm sorry. I just want to make sure that you're okay?"

I didn't answer. I was afraid I'd tell her the truth: Nothing in my life, prior to a broken heart, had hurt this bad.

Mom stared at her hands then seemed to read my mind. "It's horrible having your heart broken, especially the first time. And I hate to tell you this, but it probably won't be the last." She turned her head and looked out the window, fiddling with her wedding ring. "You're not smoking pot, are you?"

"No," I said, a little too quickly. I sat up and faced my mother, blinking back tears.

"Do you want to talk about it?"

"There's nothing to talk about," I said. "Besides, Rosie is already dating some nerd, the valedictorian who is going to Cornell with her in the fall, and she doesn't want me back."

Saying those words in such a stark way pierced my lungs like a thousand tiny pins, and the air seeped out, slow, as a sob rose in my throat. It was true: Rosie didn't want me back, and it was going to take one hell of a love song to change that. I lunged forward and hugged my mother, burying my head on her shoulder.

"It's going to be all right, honey," Mom said, rubbing the back of my head, her fingernails scratching my scalp. "It will get better."

"It hurts," I said, my words muffled.

"I know." She then pulled back, looked me in the eyes, and kissed my forehead. "Let's go out to eat."

I wiped my eyes with the hem of my t-shirt. "Can we call for take out instead?"

My mother stood and wiped the corners of her own glistening eyes. "How does pizza sound?"

"Sounds good," I said and forced a smile.

"I love you, Elliot," she said.

"Can I ask you something, Mom?"

She looked at me as if she knew what I wanted to ask. "You can ask me anything," she said.

Then I lost my nerve. "Can we get sausage instead of pepperoni?"

"Of course," Mom said. "I just want you to be happy."

I never blew on your nails, and you never knew my dreams.

I scribbled the words in a notebook on my nightstand. The line came to me after I woke from a dream where Rosie and I had spread a cotton quilt under a cloudless sky on a beach. In the dream, Rosie's long black hair was pulled into a messy bun, and she wore a white one-piece bathing suit that was so white it seemed to glow. Her bare feet were resting on my lap, and I was painting her toenails hot pink. Rosie and I used to paint each other's toes while lying on the couch and watching movies, or sitting on my bedroom floor, listening to albums. I would paint Rosie's toes then she would paint mine the same color, a secret that sometimes made me nervous when changing for gym class, but it was also slightly exciting. In the dream, after I finished painting the pinky nail on her first foot, Rosie pushed me onto my back, before I could blow on them, and straddled my lap. She kissed me so deep she sucked the breath from me.

When I woke, in those first drowsy moments that dissolve into lucidity, I believed that everything had been reconciled. Blaine McMullen was out of the picture, and we still planned to drive to Hampton Beach together on graduation night. Then, as I rubbed my eyes in the predawn light, as the neighbor's truck idled in his driveway, I remembered the truth: Rosie didn't want me back.

I picked up the phone on my nightstand and listened to the dial tone while contemplating calling her house at 5:34 a.m. Some mornings, I would call her before school, knowing she would answer on the first ring, to tell her that I loved her. But high school was over, and she was probably still asleep.

I placed the phone back in its cradle.

With that one line written in my notebook, I got up and grabbed my guitar, and for the next three hours, my love song poured from me as if a valve had opened in the place where I'd been storing the pain of my first broken heart, and the words and the chords rushed out.

Even now, as a damaged middle-aged man who has gained weight again and separated from his wife, I'd still say that "Nails" is the best song I ever wrote.

We were graduating the next morning, and that night, Rosie and Blaine McMullen and all of the Class of 1992's high-fliers attended an academic awards ceremony in the high school auditorium where they all received medals and plaques and honor cords and scholarship certificates for being generally excellent at life.

Meanwhile, after writing "Nails" then taking a long nap, I went with my friends to Bron-Yr-Aur, a clearing in the woods beside a brook that we named after a Led Zeppelin song. We'd go there to get high and drink beer. Rosie used to go there with me, although she never indulged. That night, it was me, Alan and Corky, Corky's girlfriend, Gina, a small Italian girl with a high voice and teased-up bangs that added five inches to her height, and Gina's friends, Sherry and Wendy. The six of us lived on the fringes of the high school caste system, not unpopular or ostracized—like a guy in our class named Harry Byron, who was probably busy building bombs in his basement—but also not attending the awards ceremony or invited to Craig Sandler's party at a hotel suite in downtown Manchester that his parents booked for him.

We built a small fire pit with random rocks, and as the evening sky swallowed the daylight, the dull stars appeared above us. We passed around a joint and drank a lukewarm case of Natural Light that Alan's older brother Scott bought for us at a considerable price hike. I brought my acoustic guitar with me and played a few songs where everyone knew the words and sang along.

"Did you write your love song yet, Elliot," Alan said, moving closer to Sherry on the rock where they were sitting. A trained dancer, Sherry was a lanky brunette who would blossom into a beauty, and later become a New England Patriots' cheerleader.

"I wrote something this morning," I said and took a slug of warm beer.

"Are you going to play it, dude?" Alan asked.

"It's not finished."

"Come on, Elliot," Gina said, dragging on a Newport cigarette, "I want to hear your love song."

Wendy, who was well ahead of the learning curve with a heroin-chic look—waif-thin with bobbed black hair, dark eyeliner and crimson lipstick—was sitting on a rock next to me, staring at her nails, which she had painted metallic black. "Who is it for?" she asked. "Don't tell me you wrote it for Rosie."

Eyes cast downward, I nodded. Wendy had had a crush on me since middle school, but Rosie was always in the way.

"Let's hear it," Corky said with his hand stuffed in the back pocket of Gina's acid-washed jeans.

"It's not finished," I said, strumming the guitar. While I had finished the basic chord progression—which I ripped off from a Neil Young B-side—I was still tinkering with the lyrics and fiddling with the bridge. I had planned to bring the song to band practice that week so I wasn't prepared to play it in front of people, especially girls. However, I was buzzed and stoned and heartbroken, and played an almost flawless version of the song that I wrote that morning, my voice cracking with emotion as I sang, remembering Rosie's nails.

When I finished and looked up, five faces were staring at me.

"Holy shit, dude," Alan said, breaking the silence. "That's fucking great."

Wendy lit a cigarette, her gaze burying into me. "Rosie is really lucky to have a guy like you," she said.

I shrugged. "She doesn't seem to think so."

I consumed more than I should have, seeing I was driving my mom's minivan, but I was nursing a broken heart and graduating from high school the next morning, so a little indulgence felt permissible.

I walked into the woods to take a piss with the full moon lighting my path. I leaned my shoulder against an oak tree, unzipped and tilted my head back, staring at the stars. Rosie loved astronomy. Her parents had bought her a high-powered telescope for her confirmation, and some nights, we would drive an hour into The White Mountains, and she would set up her telescope and point out the constellations to me—Andromeda and Orion and Ursa Major, Cruz and Carina. I learned more from Rosie than I had from any of the fossils who taught science at my high school.

The branches rustled behind me. Startled, I zipped quickly, spun around then stumbled forward, bumping into Wendy. She gasped. "Jesus, Elliot. You scared the shit out of me," she said, clutching her chest. At the time, I didn't realize that she had gone into the woods with the intent of finding me.

"I was looking at the stars," I said and noticed I was slurring.

"Do you remember Mrs. DeSimone's science class in middle school and that horrible slideshow on the constellations?" Wendy asked and brushed against me with her bony shoulder.

"She couldn't pronounce Cassiopeia because of her lisp."

Wendy laughed. "She hated our class."

"I sat in back of you and used to cheat off your tests," I confessed.

"I'm not sure it helped much."

I was close enough to smell her strawberry shampoo. She reached for my hand and held it. "That was a beautiful song," she said.

"You liked it?"

"I loved it," she said, her face moving toward mine. "I would absolutely melt if someone wrote that for me, and if Rosie doesn't appreciate it then she doesn't deserve you."

Our mouths met in one of those deliciously drunken teenage kisses. Other than Rosie, I had never kissed another girl at the time and knew only what I had learned from her—how much tongue to use, when to apply pressure with my lips, when to pull back. It had never occurred to me that kissing styles could differ. While Rosie was a soft kisser, Wendy was aggressive, hungry—her tongue darting past my teeth and filling my mouth. Corky was playing "Wish You Were Here" on my guitar in the distance as I grabbed Wendy's slim hips, and she ran her fingertips lightly over my crotch. We dropped slowly to the ground, onto a pile of dead leaves, and then Wendy pushed me onto my back and straddled my lap—just like my dream, only it wasn't Rosie.

I froze. "I can't," I blurted out, unsure if I meant it. My arms went limp by my sides, and I turned my head.

"You can't what?"

I stared at the stars, my head spinning. If "Nails" had this effect on Wendy, maybe Rosie would also melt and dump Blaine McMullen and take me back if she heard my pain put to music. "I'm sorry," I said to Wendy. "But I need to go."

So I left.

With a warm Natural Light in the cup holder and my guitar case in the back of the minivan, I set out for Rosie's parents' house to perform the time-honored tradition of the lover's serenade outside the maiden's bedroom window. I was lovesick and desperate with nothing to lose, the kind of situation that gives birth to some of the most heartfelt love songs.

The high beams guided me as I swerved on the winding two-lane road. Then, for no good reason, I started to sob. Maybe the booze and weed had loosened my hold on my emotions; maybe it was the image of Wendy sitting cross-legged on the ground, baffled, watching me leave; or maybe it was something more elusive, something that I couldn't seem to articulate, but I sobbed, then choked, tears blurring my vision. I turned up the radio and stepped on the gas, wiping my eyes with the back of my wrist and lifting the warm beer to my lips as I whizzed past the speed trap and the flashing lights blew up my rearview mirror.

SASQUATCH

WHILE DOING SIXTY ON A PACKED dirt road, Dad mashed a raccoon with his front tire and didn't flinch. He took a cold glance in the rearview mirror at the pile of pelt and guts then snarled.

"You're gonna roll her if you don't slow down," said Hemi, who was sandwiched between me and Dad in the cab of the pickup.

"Who are you, my wife?" Dad said. "Are you gonna tell me to clean the fucking garage next?"

Hemi glared at Dad. Although he's not a big guy, like Dad and me, Hemi is built like a crow bar, long and thin and solid—and he's no slouch with his fists. When I was twelve, I watched Hemi bust a guy's nose at a backyard barbeque, blood spouting from this poor bastard's nostrils as if shot from a hose as Hemi continued to pound his face like raw meat. He probably would've killed the guy if Dad hadn't pulled him off. Dad later told me that it was over a girl.

"This whole thing is stupid, Wayne," Hemi said.

"What whole thing?"

"This whole thing," Hemi said. "Just call the cops. She's only your stepdaughter. Let the cops deal with this punk."

Dad's eyes widened. "Only my stepdaughter? She's Darla's girl, so she's mine, too. And this 'whole thing' is a matter of her honor." Dad slammed his palms into the steering wheel. "And you don't know me from Jesus H. Christ if you think I'll let this motherfucker make a whore out of Jenny."

"We're going to end up in the clink," Hemi said under his

breath. Then he turned to me. "I hope you got enough money for bail, D.J., because your old man and me are gonna end up in the clink. Mark my word, boy. Stuffed and cuffed."

I told Hemi I only had five bucks and nothing in the bank. I blew almost all the cash I had subscribing to that porn site earlier in the week. This all happened more than a year ago and Dad and I have been through hell and back since, but to this day, I still haven't told Dad about subscribing to that site. I don't suppose I ever will.

As we zipped past a dairy farm, I stared out the window at the cows motionless in the tall grass, a full moon stamped in the night sky behind them. Everything outside the truck seemed still, like objects in a picture. Sometimes, when the night is like that, still and quiet, I try not to move. I try to fade into the background and disappear in the trees.

Dad slowed as we approached the intersection at Folger Road, where the dirt meets the pavement. He blew the stop sign then barreled left toward the Hooksett Cineplex.

I'm going to fess up now, seeing everything that happened that night at the movie theaters was—in an offhand way—my fault. Not that I did anything personally to Jenny. Not really. However, I told Dad about the website—after I subscribed— and set this whole mess into motion.

If I hadn't told Dad, none of this would've happened, and Jenny might have never left New Hampshire and vanished. And I wouldn't be here, locked up for at least a couple of years. But I had to tell him. I felt like I had no choice.

When Dad got home that Friday afternoon, Jenny was on the couch, her hand wrapped in a dishtowel packed with ice. She'd been crying, off and on, for almost a week. At first, Dad and I figured it was because Darla was back in the hospital, which was understandable. The cancer had spread to Darla's entire body, and we knew then, as hard as Darla was fighting, that she didn't have long. The doctors gave her six months, if she was lucky. She made it four months.

With Darla in the hospital, Dad had been trying to hold it together at home, but he had no idea what to do about Jenny. One night, he offered to take us to Applebee's for dinner, but Jenny didn't want to go. Then Dad went into our school to get the work Jenny had missed, but she didn't want it. Jenny didn't want to talk to Dad or me or anyone else. She just sat on the couch and cried. That afternoon, when Dad tried putting his arm around her, Jenny leaped up, punched the wall, hitting a stud, and bolted to her bedroom. Stunned, Dad rubbed his jaw like he'd been slapped. At that point, I couldn't watch it anymore. I had to tell him.

The next thing I knew, Dad called Hemi then told me to get in the truck.

I found out at school on Tuesday. Paul and I were in the back of the cafeteria, trying to ignore the chicken nuggets being launched at us—complete with the missile sound effects—from the table where the popular jocks and Jenny and the other hot girls sat, but Jenny wasn't at school. She was at home on the couch, crying.

Our own chicken nuggets, watery peas, and half-frozen potato tots lay on our trays. While lifting my brownie to my mouth, a lacrosse player with clubbed ears and curly red hair stood and snapped a picture of me with his phone. "It's Sasquatch eating a brownie!"

Sasquatch. That's what they called me. And they made up this game where they would take pictures of me doing various stuff, such as eating a brownie, or reaching into a locker for my books, or scratching my ass. Then they'd say they were sending the pictures to the Bigfoot Reporting and Research Organization. Hilarious, right?

The guys laughed at the table while the hot girls covered their mouths and pretended not to be amused by their game. It was the same damn joke, every damn day. True enough, I am six-eight and heavy-set and hairy as a buffalo—an easy target since I never fought back. Despite the fact that I was twice the size of those guys, I would sit there, still and quiet, and try to disappear. Freshman year, Coach Gallo asked me to go out for the football team, but I made up some lame excuse about a heart condition. If I could go back and change anything, I would've gone out for the football team. Then, maybe, I would've been at the other table and not ducking chicken nuggets. But it doesn't matter much now, seeing I'm not in public school anymore. I'm finishing my high school diploma here in a few months then I will probably take some college classes. I actually look forward to class. It's something to do to kill the boredom.

The truth is that I didn't play football because I was content to blend into the bleachers at the home games, as if that's possible when you're my size. Until I started seeing the white flame, I hadn't realized that, with my strength and size, I had the potential to be dangerous, a deadly weapon.

As Billy approached our table, he was tagged in the head with a chicken nugget. Billy is a hemophiliac and so pale you can see the blood running in blue streams beneath his skin. After being hit with the nugget, he didn't even turn around to look. He just placed his tray on the table and sat down as my history teacher, and the assistant football coach, pretended to yell at the jocks then ended up sitting at the table with them. Billy spit a pained look at me. "I heard something," he said. "About your stepsister."

"I know what it is," Paul said with a jack-o-lantern grin. When Paul smiles, his fat cheeks scrunch around his bucked teeth and you want to smack that look straight off his face. Paul got a late jump on puberty and, at sixteen, he was still as hairless as a clenched fist. "I heard it, too," he said.

"What the hell are you talking about?" I said.

Before I go any further, before I disclose everything, you have to know this: my stepsister was *hot*. I mean, smoking *hot*. She was still hot when she disappeared after everything happened, and I assume, wherever she is now, she is still hot today.

Now before you judge me, which some of you are going to do anyway, try to remember that I was a sixteen-year-old guy and not blood-related, living in the same house with a hot girl. And it is not like we'd lived together all our lives, like real siblings. Jenny and Darla had moved in with Dad and me only two years before. It happened fast. Dad met Darla during my freshman year, and a few months later, they were married, and this hot chick from school was prancing around the house in slinky tops and yoga shorts. Listen, I'm not proud of this, but let's just say, I could still draw you a full-color diagram of her underwear drawer.

"What the hell are the two of you talking about?" I asked, stabbing a chicken nugget with my fork. Paul and Billy stared at each other, both biting their bottom lips. I'd had enough games. I saw the white flame. "Tell me what you know, or I'm going to bust open both your mouths," I said.

The guys stiffened like they were bracing for a punch, then Billy coughed weakly into his sleeve. "You know that guy your stepsister has been dating," Billy said, "that Marine guy who works at the movie theaters?"

"Mike."

Billy nodded. "I heard he put some, um, videos of your stepsister on a website." When Billy blushed, his entire face and neck turned bright red, like a fresh blood stain on a hospital sheet.

My face, on the other hand, was a blank screen. The only thing I could think about was getting to that website. I know, I know. I'm sick and perverted and I probably belong in this cell, but that's what I thought. "What's the name of the site?"

Billy frowned. "Why would I know? It's not like I'm looking at that stuff."

"*Black Market Sex Tapes*," said Paul. "You have to subscribe to see the whole thing, but you can watch the clips for free. I heard she takes on two guys at the same time."

I didn't want to believe it, but I didn't doubt it.

Although it pains me to think about him, I suppose I should tell you about Jenny's ex-boyfriend Mike. The newspapers, which have been covering the story since it happened, say there's a chance he'll walk again, which is good, I guess. Not that it matters much to me. I'm already doing three years for aggravated assault, and then I'll be up for parole.

Mike went to the same regional high school Jenny and I attended, graduating five years before I got there. But that doesn't matter much. We all know his type: the handsome, popular guy who is in all the yearbook pictures and dates all the hot girls. You know him—the King of Cool, the big man on campus, smooth as an oil slick. He had it all until the end of his senior year when one of the hot girls accused him of rape, and the next thing you know, two other girls came forward. One was underage, so with the statutory charge tacked on, Mike was looking at doing some serious time—he could've been here instead of me—then the three girls backed off and refused to testify. Without witnesses or evidence, the charges were thrown out.

As soon as he was cleared, Mike enlisted in the Marines and went off to Parris Island then was shipped somewhere in the Middle East. Afghanistan, I think. When he returned, the town gave him the hero's welcome. He walked in the Fourth of July parade in his dress blues. He was, again, The King of Cool and he went back to work as a manager at the movie theaters in Hooksett. A year ago, when the newspapers were first running those articles on Mike—when he was "the veteran fighting for his life"—the date rape accusations were never mentioned, nor was the fact that he sold his sex tapes of him and his buddy tag-teaming my drunk and roofied stepsister to a porn site. Those stories had completely vanished.

Another chicken nugget was launched at our table, but this time I reached up and caught it in the air, crushing it in my hand. The white flame flickered. I stood up with my arm cocked, ready to shove that chicken nugget down someone's throat when Mr. Nagle, the vice-principal, tapped me on the shoulder.

"What are you planning to do with that chicken nugget, Mr. Briggs?" he asked. He was this small leprechaun-type, bald with two tufts of reddish hair and pointed ears. I could've broken him in half.

"Nothing," I said.

"Give me the nugget, son," he said and held out his hand. I dropped it in his palm. "I don't want to see any more trouble from you, you hear?"

"Yes, sir," I said.

Billy and Paul were staring at me in awe. "Were you really going to throw that at them?" Paul asked, flashing that jack-o-lantern grin.

"Shut up, Paul," I said and flicked a pea at his head.

"I'm gonna feed this prick his fucking teeth," Dad said, reaching into his coat pocket and removing a pint of Southern Comfort. After a swig, he passed the bottle to Hemi. "It's been awhile since I've given someone a good ass-kicking."

"When was the last time we scrapped, Wayne?"

"A couple of years, at least. The last one I remember was in that dive bar in Manchester, when those hipster cocksuckers in those skinny jeans started with us."

In the dull glow of the dashboard, Dad's lips relaxed and a small smile formed. If I could go back and freeze that night, it would be right there: Dad smiling in his truck's dashboard lights and maybe, for a second, considering turning around.

As we stopped at the light where the two left lanes turned into the Cineplex, a blue sedan pulled up beside us. Inside, Jameson Racine, a halfback on the football team, was driving with his girl, Amber St. Lawrence, in the passenger seat, her arm hanging out the window. Jameson turned, looked at me, and nudged her.

"It's Sasquatch riding in a truck," he said and pointed. Amber didn't bother to turn her head. But that didn't stop Jameson from getting out his cell phone and snapping a picture. "Sasquatch, smile."

I rolled up the window. Behind my eyes, the white flame flickered, and I ripped the pint from Hemi's hand. I wasn't used to drinking, so the liquor, as I poured a mouthful down my throat, made me cough and gag.

"What the hell do you think you're doing?" Dad asked.

"Sorry."

"What did that guy call you?" Hemi jerked his thumb in the direction of the blue sedan.

"I didn't hear him."

Dad tilted his head and looked at me like he was doing math. The light changed, but we didn't move. The cars behind us started honking. I stared at the floorboards, the pint still in my sweaty hand.

"Pass that bottle over here," Dad said.

As I handed him the pint, the man in the car behind us stuck his arm out the window and threw the middle finger at Dad. Without turning around, Dad launched the near-empty bottle out the window at the guy's car, missing it by a bunch as it smashed on the concrete. Dad hit the gas.

I went straight home after school to find the website. Most days, I'd stop at the Hess station and pick up a two-liter of Mountain Dew and a bag of Cool Ranch Doritos. Sometimes I'd stick around the store and flip through the magazines or play some scratch tickets. They never carded me, even for beer. Before she started dating Mike, Jenny used to ask me to buy booze for her and her friends before they'd go to parties. To tell you the truth, I liked doing it. While I was putting those bottles of liquor in the trunks of their cars, and the girls were thanking me and brushing my arm with their bird-bone fingers, I was a part of their world. But it never lasted. Since my purpose was clear, my presence in their company was strange and slightly awkward, and I'd quickly vanish from the picture. Seen for an instant then gone.

When I got home that afternoon, Jenny was lying on the couch, holding the remote control with her arm outstretched and crumpled tissues scattered like shotgun shells on the carpet. I stood in the living room, as still and dumb as a bear rug.

"Are you all right?" I asked Jenny.

"Let me guess. You heard." She stared straight at the television, pale and zombie-like, surfing through Netflix.

"I don't know what you're talking about."

"You wouldn't."

With my head down, I went straight to my bedroom, locking the door behind me. I opened my laptop and went to the *Black Market Sex Tapes* website. On the homepage, in a still-frame from a grainy video taken on a phone, a drunken Jenny forced a smile. My heart stammered, my erection throbbed, my breathing became labored, and I took the bankcard from my wallet.

There was Planet Fitness and a Target in the same plaza as the movie theater, and the parking lot was packed on Friday night. We found a spot in the back, beneath a floodlight. Dad cut the engine.

"Let's fuck him up," he said, his voice watery. Being a large man, it takes a lot of booze to faze Dad, but he had been drinking since coming home that afternoon, even before I told him about the website. I'm not sure what Dad thought was going to happen, but he had to know that it wasn't going to end well.

A few parking spaces down from us, Jameson and Amber got out of the blue sedan. When I looked over, Jameson snapped another picture—Sasquatch walking into a movie theater. Maybe that sip of Southern Comfort hit me harder than I realized because I slung my middle finger at Jameson and snarled like Dad snarled when he ran over the raccoon. And wouldn't you know it—Jameson put his phone in his pocket and looked the other way.

"What's that all about?" Dad asked.

"Some asshole from school."

The line to buy the tickets wrapped around the side of the building. As we walked past the line, a couple of guys yelled out, "Sasquatch!"

The white flame burned as I balled my fists.

When we got in the lobby, Dad stopped me. "What were those guys calling you?"

"Sasquatch, Dad. They call me Sasquatch."

"And you put up with it?"

I shrugged. When Dad looked at me, it was as if my skin was

made of glass and he could see through me into the hollowed-out shell where my guts should've been. For the first time, it was as if he understood that he had failed to raise a man.

Hemi clamped me on the shoulder. "I'm not sure if you know this or not, D.J., but you could wipe your ass with those guys. Crack one skull and the rest will back off."

"There's that motherfucker." Dad pointed at a muscular guy with short black hair, heavily gelled and sleeves of tattoos on both arms that I recognized from the website. He was collecting ticket stubs. With Hemi and me behind him, Dad pushed through the crowd. When he arrived at the entrance to the theaters, cordoned off by a thick purple rope, he positioned himself in front of Mike, dwarfing him by at least a foot. Dad stared down at him like a boxer receiving instructions, breathing through his nostrils.

Mike looked at him as if Dad were a skinny bird flapping its wings. "Back off, big fella," Mike said.

"Do you know who I am?" Dad said.

"I know who you are," said Mike.

As murmurs of a fight caught fire in the lobby, everyone's attention shifted toward Dad and Mike. That's when something started to grind inside me, waiting to explode through my skin. My legs shook. The white flame pounded behind my eyes.

"Is there a problem?" Mike asked in a flat, steady voice.

"Yeah," said Dad, bumping him with his chest, "there's a big fucking problem."

Dad pulled back and swung at Mike's head. Mike ducked it, and before anyone could blink, he had Dad's arm bent behind his back, ready to snap it. Dad screamed.

That scream was the last thing that registered.

■■■

When the security cop and another employee pulled me

off Mike, my fists and forearms were covered in his blood. Mike lay like a sack of sand on the ground. I remember a lot of screaming and shouting. As I was being wrestled to my stomach and restrained, I looked for Dad, but couldn't find him.

"What the hell got into Sasquatch?" I heard someone say. And someone else said, "I don't know, but I think he fucking killed that guy." Then another voice said, "You had to see that coming."

I closed my eyes and made myself real still, careful not to move, then disappeared.

AMERICA THE GREAT

AVA BLINKED BACK TEARS WHILE staring at her parents' house on Long Creek Road from the back of the blue van. She grew up in that house—a five-bedroom, three-story Colonial with an in-ground swimming pool and a cabana in the backyard—and before she moved into the van with Mickey, it was the only place where she had ever lived.

Mickey tugged at his patchy beard as he watched the guests enter through a gate in the picket fence. "Is there anything more American than gouging yourself on commercially farmed beef on the Fourth of July then getting your rocks off on the fireworks in your backyard when it gets dark?"

"Probably not," Ava said and forced a tight-lipped smile.

Gordon Lightfoot's "Sundown" played from the pool-area, alongside the low chatter of the guests and the excited screams of kids playing in the water. Ava glanced at the new Minnie Mouse tattoo on her forearm that Mickey had done for her two nights before, the skin swollen and red around the ink, possibly infected. The closer she looked at the tattoo, the more it appeared that Minnie Mouse was suffering from Bell's palsy. Mickey fanned his hand in front of his face, waiting for traces.

"Why did you take that acid?" Ava asked him.

"It gives me perspective when dealing with fascists," he said. "I'm pretty sure none of these MAGA assholes are going to like me anyway, so fuck them. Fuck them and their bourgeois bullshit."

"They are my parents and their friends," Ava mumbled. "And my mom is a Democrat. She voted for Kamala."

"They're all fucking fascists."

Ava looked again at her house. It had been five weeks since she graduated from high school, and three months since she met Mickey at a house party where he had bought all the booze and was illegally tattooing drunken teenagers in the basement for cash. At the time, Ava was still dating Chase, the son of her parents' best friends, and she couldn't quite explain her attraction to Mickey, who resembled a young, taller Charlie Manson. But she fell for him and fell for him hard, and a week later, Ava broke it off with Chase, who she had been dating for four years. Then, three weeks ago, she tried moving Mickey into her bedroom at her parents' house, and when her parents refused—her father told Mickey that he wasn't welcome there to get a job—Ava moved into Mickey's blue van, where they parked at Walmart each night, surviving on Ava's graduation money and the little cash Mickey made doing tattoos and selling his Adderall prescription.

A plump, sun-burned couple that Ava recognized from her church waddled past the blue van, the man carrying a cooler while his wife cradled a plastic bowl of potato salad.

"Look at that, baby girl," Mickey said and pointed at the couple. "That's everything that is wrong with this shit-toast country. Look at those twat waffles going to stuff their fat faces."

Ava sensed one of Mickey's Antifa rants rumbling and tried to cut it off by rubbing his thigh, nuzzling his neck and recoiling slightly at his stench. "By tomorrow morning, we'll be leaving all of this behind," she said.

"With a shitload of your dad's cash," Mickey said and placed his hand over Ava's. "I think the acid is kicking in."

Ava pushed him onto his back and straddled his lap. "We need to hurry then," she said.

Mickey unzipped his cargo shorts. "God Bless America."

■■■

The sun beat down from a cloudless sky. In the backyard, a group of rail-thin middle school boys cannon-balled into the pool, splashing a group of girls who screamed at them from the shallow end; bored wives in their floppy-brimmed sun hats and oversized sunglasses sat poolside beneath an umbrella in a rainbow array of sarongs and sundresses, sipping sangria and confiding their secret lusts for the college boys home for the summer. Meanwhile, their beer-bellied husbands palmed cold beers and played Cornhole on the lawn, wearing wrap-around shades, their tribal band tattoos fading on their biceps like old wishes.

Ava's father manned the grill on the raised deck, holding his spatula like a sword. In his mid-forties, Brad was barrel-chested and bearded, his head shaved to the scalp to disguise his receding hairline. Beside him, Aaron, Chase's father, drank a tall gin and tonic while scrolling through his phone.

Aaron was the first to notice Ava and Mickey walk through the gate with their dirty clothes and tangled hair, beach sandals and the cheap plastic sunglasses that Mickey shoplifted from a drugstore. They looked like they had escaped from Spahn Ranch, and when people started to notice them, the chatter dimmed to whispers.

"We're in enemy territory, baby girl," Mickey said as they approached the deck.

"It'll be fine," Ava said, squeezing his hand.

As she began up the deck stairs toward her father, Ava let go of Mickey's hand and bounded up the steps. Once on the landing, she ran toward her father, throwing her arms around him. Ava hadn't contacted him in a week, ignoring his texts. "I missed you," she said.

Brad pulled his only child into his chest. "I've missed you, too, kiddo," he said and backed up and held her at arm's length.

When he saw the tattoo, he frowned and pointed to her forearm. "What the hell is that? Is that real?"

"Not now, Dad."

"Did that piece of shit do that to you? Tell him to get off my property before I rip off his dick and feed it to him in a hot dog roll."

"We don't want trouble, Dad. I just want everyone to get along."

"When are you coming home, Ava?"

"Can we talk about this later?"

Brad looked into his daughter's eyes, the same bright blue as his own. He couldn't understand any of it—why she left or what she saw in this filthy man. She and Chase were the homecoming king and queen that fall. She had been accepted, early-admissions, into Northeastern, and Chase had received a baseball scholarship to Boston College. The young couple's future seemed predestined, sealed with their parents' approval. Then Mickey—the unemployed tattoo artist who couldn't draw—appeared like some ineluctable force of nature, a natural disaster, and, suddenly, his daughter changed into something unrecognizable to him.

After spotting Ava from her poolside perch, her mother Amy jumped up and ran toward her, passing Mickey on the deck stairs without acknowledgement.

"Minnie," Amy cried. It was her nickname for Ava. When Ava was an infant, she looked exactly like a picture of her mother at the same age—the nickname was short for "Mini-me" and something Ava secretly liked. Amy was still a handsome youthful-looking woman in her mid-forties, and the mother and daughter could've passed for sisters.

Ava rushed to her mother as Mickey made his way up the landing, grinning. Brad crossed his arms, staring steely-eyed at

Mickey. "You look lost," Brad said to him. "Do you need me to show you the way out?"

"Chill, man. We just stopped for a bite to eat," Mickey said, unfazed.

"Try getting a job and buying your own damn food, you fucking bum," Brad said.

"Dad!"

"Brad, please," Amy snapped. "Ava is an adult, and we need to respect her decisions, even if we don't agree with them."

Mickey threw up his arms. "I'm bouncing, baby girl. I don't want to be around these fascist assholes."

Ava watched with horror as her boyfriend headed back down the deck stairs. "Don't leave without me," Ava screamed.

"Don't you worry. I'll wait for you forever," he called back. "I love you."

"I love you, too," Ava yelled then stared at her parents.

Her mother grabbed both of Ava's hands. "Please don't go. Stay and have something to eat. Please, Minnie."

Brad placed a hand on Ava's small shoulder. "Please, honey."

Ava twirled a strand of greasy hair around her finger. She had to stick around the house that night in order to execute with their plan anyway. "I think I'm going to take a shower," she said, her stomach hurting.

"I miss you, Minnie," Amy said.

Ava took a deep breath and exhaled, her heart torn. "I miss you, too," she said. "I'm going to take a shower now."

The walls in Ava's bedroom were painted a pale pink, and there were hanging shelves made of solid oak that Brad built for a porcelain doll collection that Ava inherited from his mother. The dolls stood on the shelves like a mute choir with their bowed mouths and their high blush and their bushels of fake hair.

Ava walked into her bathroom and realized that her mother had cleaned it as if she had anticipated her return. After running a hot shower, she stepped out of her filthy jean shorts and removed her tank top, depositing them in a wicker hamper, followed by her dirty bra and panties. She stood beneath the shower head, as hot water streamed through her hair and massaged her scalp. She then stared down at the Minnie Mouse tattoo with a wave of regret before carefully soaping and cleaning it. It definitely looked infected, she decided. It was her first tattoo, and she knew that she couldn't get it fixed without insulting Mickey. She knew there were decisions to be made.

The three hard thumps on the bathroom door startled her. "Who is it?" she called from behind the curtain.

"It's the Deep State."

Ava stuck her head out from the shower and saw him, steam-blurred, standing in the doorway. "How did you get in? You need to get out of here. My father will literally kill you if he finds you here. He owns guns!"

"What a surprise, the fascist owns guns," Mickey said and plopped down, cross-legged, his back against the doorway. "I found that ladder on the side of the house and climbed up, but I'm not sure I can get down. I'm tripping balls, baby girl."

"One minute," said Ava and quickly washed her hair and soaped up a loofah, a hurried process that curtailed her fantasy of a long, hot shower.

After toweling off, she threw on the pink terrycloth bathrobe hanging on the back of the door then sat on the edge of the bed next to Mickey, who was staring at a framed photo of Ava and her friends in the bleachers at a football game. "I forget that you were a cool kid," he said.

"A lot of my friends no longer speak to me. They think I've lost my mind."

"That's because their minds are small, and they can't see the big picture," Mickey said then he pointed to the porcelain dolls on the shelves. "Those things are freaking me out."

"My grandmother gave them to me."

"No one has ever given me shit," Mickey said and boyishly folded his hands in his lap and stared at the floor. "Actually, that's not true. My mom made me a Ninja Turtles blanket for Christmas the year my dad left. We were broke, and she sewed it herself. It was the only gift I got. She might still have it somewhere."

Ava placed her hand lightly on Mickey's cheek. "I'll bet she does," she said.

Then someone knocked on the bedroom door. Wide-eyed, Ava and Mickey looked at each other. "I'm getting dressed," Ava called in a shaky voice.

"Is it all right if I come in?" It was her mother. "I need to talk to you, Minnie."

"Get in the bathroom," Ava hissed at Mickey. "Get in the tub. Pull the shower curtain closed and don't make a sound."

Mickey nodded then he tip-toed into the bathroom, softly closing the door behind him. "Come in," Ava yelled.

Her mother entered and stood in the center of the room. She looked Ava in the eyes, smiling plaintively. "I'm happy you came home."

"Mom, I can explain."

"I understand," her mother said.

"I don't think you do," Ava said. "I've never felt like this about a guy before, not even Chase. With Chase, it was pretend love. But this is real, Mom."

Her mother sat on the edge of the bed beside her. "I was in love with a guy in college and almost gave up everything for him. His name was Ben, and he played guitar in a band that was popular in the bars around campus. We thought they were going to be the next Pearl Jam, and I followed him around like a puppy dog, doing whatever he wanted me to do, forgetting about my friends. My whole world revolved around Ben. Ben this. Ben that. I get it. You're infatuated."

"It's love, Mom, not infatuation."

"Sometimes it's hard to tell the difference."

"I know the difference," Ava said defiantly. They sat in silence for a few moments until Ava broke it. "So what happened?"

Her mother took a deep breath and closed her eyes, as if summoning a ghost. "I was going to quit school and move with him to Boston. He had rented a cheap place in Somerville, and all of my things were packed in the moving van, ready to go. The night before we were going to move, I found him in bed with my roommate, Gwen. Ben and Gwen. Cute, right? They ended up getting married."

"Mickey would never cheat on me." Ava looked at the bathroom door.

"That's not my point, Minnie."

"Then what is your point? It's not like you're an expert on love. No offense, Mom, but you and Dad hardly talk."

Her mother nodded. "Marriage is hard."

Ava rolled her eyes. "What is your point?"

"Slow things down," she said. "Move back home for awhile and think about things. Think about going to Northeastern in the fall. You worked so hard to get into that school, and you still have your dorm assignment. Think about it, Minnie. And then if you still want to be with that boy, you should."

"He's not a boy."

"Yes, he is." Amy stood and kissed her daughter on the forehead then paused and glared at the bathroom door. "I love you," she said.

"I love you, too," said Ava.

When the door closed, Mickey snuck out from the bathroom. "Your hair dryer was talking to me, baby girl, speaking in Arabic. Imagine that. The hair dryer in Captain America's house is an Islamic terrorist."

"I wish you hadn't taken that acid," Ava said.

Mickey came over to the bed and placed his arms around her waist. "By this time tomorrow, we'll be fucking on a king-sized bed in an expensive hotel on our way to California."

With the central air conditioning blasting in the bedroom, neither of them heard the first string of firecrackers popping on the concrete below the deck.

A lacquered wooden sign with "Brad's Billiards" burned into the oak hung on the far wall. One Christmas morning, when Ava was in middle school, she and her mother had lugged the sign—heavy enough that it required both of them to carry it—twenty yards from the garage, where it was half-heartedly hidden beneath a bed sheet, to the billiards' room, which Brad was building in the basement. After Ava finished opening her presents, she and her mother led Brad downstairs to see his gift, which was leaning against a table saw. Brad chuckled, kissed Ava on the forehead and her mother on the mouth. As far as Ava could remember, it was the last time that she saw her parents kiss.

The billiards room was now finished with a cedar bar, three stools, and a red-felted pool table in the center. It smelled of stale cigar smoke, a sweet smell that Ava found vaguely nostalgic and not entirely unpleasant as she entered the room, using the flashlight on her phone to see in front of her. She knew the floor safe was underneath the pool table, covered by an area rug. She had stumbled upon the combination one night, about a year before, when she and Chase were shooting pool. Ava dropped an earring while grabbing a ginger ale from the mini-fridge beneath the bar and discovered a list of numbers taped underneath the bar top. Quickly figuring out what the numbers were, she and Chase moved the rug and opened the safe, discovering stacks of cash in rubber bands, envelopes and folders with official documents, as well as a lock box containing her mother's heirloom jewelry.

In the dark, Ava found the combination again, copying the numbers onto a piece of scrap paper then moving the rug, punching in the combination, and opening the safe. The inside looked unchanged with the stacks of hundred dollar bills, although the pile seemed to be larger. Brad distrusted banks, and Ava knew the cash was a large portion of their life's savings, and someday her inheritance.

She stared at the money and paused, her backpack open beside her. Her limbs wouldn't move as the tears she had blinked back that afternoon streamed down the sides of her face. Everything she'd done in the three-month whirlwind with Mickey spun like a tornado ripping through her, and she realized that she couldn't go through with it. She had too much to lose. Ava closed the latch and covered the safe with the rug.

According to their plan, Mickey would be waiting in the cabana for her to return with the backpack full of cash. He would be disappointed, possibly angry with her when she told him about her decision. And what exactly was she going to tell him? How would he react when she told him that she didn't want to drive to California with him, and she wanted to move back home? She certainly didn't want him driving on acid in the middle of night, so she thought that maybe she would wait until the morning to have that talk.

Ava followed the flashlight's beam out of the billiards room, through the basement and into the backyard. She had turned off the motion detectors and followed the light into the pool area, heading toward the cabana where he'd be waiting. As she walked barefoot on a strip of cool cement, the black water rippled in the moonlight from an object floating beneath the diving board. She moved closer, pointing the light in its direction. The body was facedown, its arms spread in a crucifix pose, the long hair splayed on the water's surface. Ava vomited in the water and wiped her mouth before catching her breath, tilting back her head and releasing a scream that could be heard from sea to shining sea.

Part II

THE MAN OF THE HOUSE

THE MAN WHO IS FUCKING MY WIFE is a cowboy—not a Top Forty country music cowboy, but a horseback, dust-and-grit-between-his-teeth *cowboy*. He's strong-jawed and quiet, capable of answering a compound question with a brusque nod or a slight grin—never anything polysyllabic. He only shaves on weekends and makes Old Spice smell nostalgic. The sun has given his skin a tight, leathered look, and when he smiles—which isn't often—it stretches his face like a belt.

The man who is fucking my wife has a chest like John Wayne and dons a duster like Clint Eastwood. He votes a straight Republican ticket and makes no apologies for it. He sees social issues as things that people need to fix for themselves and speaks in conservative clichés: "There's no such thing as a free ride" or "You can't help someone who won't help themselves." He has a way of making even bleeding heart women, such as my wife, believe things were better when we all rode horses.

The man who is fucking my wife is the American cowboy paradigm; he wears the white hat in Westerns; his top lip never quivers after a shot of Wild Turkey; he keeps a toothpick in the corner of his mouth and flips it with his tongue; he expects a full ten minutes of head before sex.

The man who is fucking my wife has a gargantuan cock, a cock that coils in his shorts and impresses a distinctive bulge in his tight-fitting blue jeans. He's no enigma. When my wife unzips his fly and reaches into his briefs, her eyes widen and she wets her lips. She looks him in the eyes and says, "My, my."

■■■

My God, she's beautiful, I think as Lisa walks into the kitchen and places a cardboard box on the counter.

I shake two pills into my palm and wash them down with tepid coffee. I had a car accident in my mid-twenties and have since had chronic back pain. It's legitimate. Despite what my wife may believe, my back bothers me daily, especially when it rains.

It's a breezy day in May, and Lisa shakes her head as I tuck the pill bottle back in my pocket. Nabbed. It doesn't matter. She's beautiful when she's disappointed, too. It's such a damn shame that she's cheating on me.

"Moving must be really painful, Mark."

"More than you know." I take a quarter from my pocket and start to practice The Disappearing Coin, a sleight of hand trick that I learned years ago when my parents divorced and I took up magic. I was never any good at it, so I stopped for many years, and only recently decided, on a whim, that I want to perfect the trick, and now it is almost a nervous tick.

Lisa sits across from me at the kitchen table, the first large piece of furniture we brought into the new house. It's a sturdy slab of shellacked oak that came with four matching chairs, a wedding gift from my mother and stepfather. The legs need tightening. It's nothing I can't fix with an Allen wrench, but right now, we're just trying to get the U-haul unloaded. We only moved twenty miles from the west side of Manchester into the sticks in Candia and thought we'd save money by moving ourselves. Big mistake. In fact, we wouldn't be moving at all if Lisa hadn't decided that we needed to own a house. She argued, rightfully, that we'd build equity instead of throwing money away on rent. But our mortgage is almost double what we were paying in rent, and I liked our little two-bedroom place. Sure, it was small and damp and the roof leaked every once in a while, but it was comfortable. Besides, I'm not a big fan of major life changes.

The whole move, by the way, was orchestrated by Lisa's parents. We've been married four years now, and according to Frank and Nora Weiss—the consummate authorities on everything—married couples should own a house. End of discussion.

Three days ago, we closed on this renovated farmhouse on the top of a hill, with only one neighbor whose house is thirty yards away, near the bottom of our driveway. Now we're hauling furniture and cardboard boxes, and there was no one available to help us. All of our friends—and I don't have many, except my childhood best friend Geoff, who lives in Sacramento—were conveniently busy. Lisa could've asked her boyfriend to help us move the big stuff—at least the bed, where he has some vested interest.

Did I mention that Lisa is cheating on me?

I smile at her, waiting for the Percocet to spread like oil through my limbs and the floating to take hold. Meanwhile, I practice my trick. I hold up the coin for Lisa. "Now you see it," I say and swipe my hand across the coin then show her my open palms. "Now you don't."

"If you take any more of those pills, we're going to have to rent the U-Haul for another day," Lisa says, taking out her ponytail and letting her blonde hair spill down her back.

I look at her face in the sunlight. My wife's face is a study in symmetry, a sharp nose and high cheekbones. She modeled for a short time in college, some catalogues and bathing suit ads, but she said it made her feel cheap and quit. Now she'll occasionally write some freelance articles for some of the publications where her ads once ran.

I'll be the first to admit I married outside of my league.

I out-kicked my coverage, as the saying goes. At my wedding, after slugging back a dozen or so whiskey sours, my real father, who was a drunken asshole before cancer got him, put his hand on my shoulder—more to keep himself upright than a paternal pat—and said, "Son, keep your eye on this one. She's a beautiful woman, and you, unfortunately, look like me." Sadly, my looks are not the only thing that I inherited from him.

Lisa stands up to continue unpacking and shrieks. One hand is covering her chest as the other points out the bay windows in the kitchen at the neighbor's house at the bottom of the hill. "The neighbors are pulling a camper into their yard."

There's a white RV trailer plopped like a dead body on the strip of crab grass that separates our driveways. "So what," I say and make the coin disappear again.

"So what?" she says. "Do you know what this means? We've moved next to rednecks. No wonder we got this house so cheap. We should've listened to my parents and met the neighbors before making an offer. Now we're living next to the dueling banjos. They're going to be riding four-wheelers around the property and firing off guns and raising chickens."

"Just because they have a camper doesn't mean they are rednecks."

Lisa reaches in her pocketbook on the counter for her cigarettes. "My parents will never let us hear the end of it."

Unlike my mom and stepfather, who now live outside Tampa, the Weisses live only half an hour away in Hooksett, where I grew up. My body starts to slouch in the chair as my head starts to nod back, the oil spreading through my veins.

"Mark!"

I snap awake. "I'm here."

"We need to finish unloading the truck," she says and storms out of the kitchen, one long stalk of leg in front of the next. I try to imagine those legs wrapped around another man's bare back, but the pills are taking hold now. All is well.

"Did you come in me?"

"No. I don't think so. I mean, maybe. Yes."

"I told you I didn't have my diaphragm in." Lisa takes a cigarette from a pack on her dresser.

"You could've stopped me."

"I'm so sorry, Captain Percocet. I didn't realize that it was my job."

Lisa rolls off the bed and grabs one of my t-shirts from the floor. I turn my head and stare at the glowing red digits on the alarm clock. It's after midnight, but my pill bottle blocks my full view of the clock. I reach across the bed for my pills and shake one from the bottle.

"Have another one," Lisa quips.

"I will," I say and dry swallow the pill.

Lisa is now standing at the foot of the bed, her silhouette hovering over me like a deadline. I close my eyes and wait to be carried to sleep, the oil spreading from my chest to one limb at a time.

"I have too much I want to do to get pregnant."

"You sound like your parents."

"Fuck you."

Immediately, I wish I could take it back, shove those words back into my big mouth and swallow them like fist-sized pills.

In the twelve years that I've known Lisa, she has always worked hard to cultivate an image of herself as her parents' antithesis—working for a local newspaper, voting for Democrats, marrying me when she was twenty-eight. Nevertheless, some of their qualities—for example, the need for the world to exist, without exception, according to their own demands and designs—could not be side-stepped. Lisa won't admit to it, but it's sometimes hard to see what is directly in front of you. She couldn't shake the Weiss' Puritanical drive to work into the ground, and she couldn't completely shake their pretension. All the Weisses are that way, from her asshole attorney father, to her power suit corporate cunt mom, to her bitch-on-overdrive older sister, who has her own plastic surgery practice and married a Wall Street stockbroker. Lisa is—in the words of her mother— "just a reporter covering school board meetings." The ostensible is everything to Weisses, and writing local news stories for a paltry salary for the past decade is not glamorous or prestigious enough. So when Lisa upped and married the college dropout who writes computer code from home after dating him for eight years, the Weisses shit serious bricks. Not only do I not fit the avaricious blond-haired Aryan model of a husband they had in mind for their daughter, but I am also a marquee member of a group they find to be the most reprehensible subclass of the human species: the pacifistic beta male, and now, apparently, a cuckold, too. The thought of Lisa bearing my child would send a shot of pure terror up their already stiff spines.

Lisa is still standing at the foot of the bed, a ribbon of cigarette smoke rising from her limp right hand. Suddenly, she is standing in a stranger's bedroom. I see him on the bed, sitting upright with his arm hugging the headboard, his own cigarette dangling from his lips. The man beckons her with his index finger and tells to get her "sweet ass" back in bed.

The room swarms.

"I'm sorry," I say and lunge for the lamp on the nightstand, flicking it on. Lisa tilts her head, looking at me as if she is trying to place my face from an old yearbook. Slowly, the mask of annoyance crumbles like dried dirt wiped from the surface of a precious stone. She sits down on the edge of the bed and runs her fingers through my hair.

"I'm sorry, too," she says and lies down with her back to me, looking out the bedroom window at the dim hint of stars. "On the drive into work the other day, when it started pouring, I started thinking about that time in Wyoming when we were camping and that storm came in."

"I remember," I say. "It was Montana. We spent the night before in that filthy motel in Missoula."

"Right."

It was the summer before our senior year at the University of New Hampshire, two years before my car accident. I was still straddling the fence about whether to drop out of school and go to work for a friend who was offering me a salary that was hard to pass up. Lisa and I had quit our summer jobs at a restaurant in Dover and took my Toyota Corolla from New Hampshire to Colorado where Geoff worked as a firefighter in Fort Collins at the time. Afterwards, instead of heading back East on I-70, we turned north on I-25 and decided to spend a few weeks following the winds.

We bought a tent at Target and camped beside a picturesque lake in a state park in Montana for the night. The next morning was humid, our skin damp and sticky. We made love on top of a flannel sleeping bag, sweating inside the tent's taffeta walls. Afterwards, I lay on top of Lisa, my head resting on her bare breasts. Suddenly, the barometric pressure dropped like a metal ball down a fiberglass chute. A vicious clap of thunder shook the ground. Lisa screamed, and I covered her body with my own as torrential rains pelted the tent. Truth be told, I was scared shitless, having never experienced such a sudden and surly storm, but I kept my fears in check so Lisa would feel protected.

Now, I can't even keep her for myself. I reach over Lisa and grab another Percocet from the bottle on the nightstand. She sighs as I turn off the lamp.

"My parents are coming for dinner on Friday," she says. "They want to see the new house."

"You shouldn't get me so excited. I'll never get to sleep."

"Have another pill."

"I will," I say and place a hand on Lisa's belly. What if my sperm—right at this moment—is bull-charging an egg, ready to strike, but some other man's sperm is already there? "Sorry, chump," his sperm will say to my own. "You can turn around now."

"Montana," I whisper as I finally start to nod off.

Allow me to describe the dinner scene where Frank and Nora Weiss visit Mark Fellini and his beautiful wife Lisa Weiss.

Frank, in a well-pressed suit, and Nora, in a long skirt and a blouse—attire designed to offer a clear juxtaposition with Mark, who wears faded blue jeans and a white "Steal Your Face" t-shirt—will arrive ten minutes before seven o'clock. Lisa will have prepared a thoughtful and health-conscious entrée of baked salmon with a cucumber cream sauce. The four of them will dine to the sounds of silverware scratching the fine china—a wedding gift from the Weisses—interspersed with terse spits of conversation.

Sometime after dessert—a tiramisu from a small Italian market in Manchester—Frank, having spotted a camper at the bottom of the driveway, will level a cutting criticism at his daughter for not talking to the neighbors before buying the house, thus opening the flood gates for Nora to sound off like a Greek chorus. Thus begins a complete verbal evisceration of their daughter while Mark, who will drink too much wine compounded with four Percocets—one of which he smoked off a strip of foil in the new basement—will tune out.

The evening will eventually end with a cold goodnight, then

Lisa and Mark will continue to drink entirely too much and say things that they will never get back, or forget.

Two bottles of Chardonnay are empty and the dinner candles have burned down to waxy nubs when Lisa starts talking about her editor, some faceless big dick named Ron who used to work at *The Boston Globe*. I have never met Ron, nor been invited to meet Ron. Ron is from Cambridge. Ron is a wife-fucker's name if I've ever heard a wife-fucker's name. So I blurt out, "Are you fucking Ron?"

Her eyes widen and mouth drops open. "What are you talking about?"

"You know, Ron. Are you and Ronny getting hot and heavy on the editor's desk? Is Ron giving you the big Ron-bone?"

"You need to lay off the pills." She lights a cigarette off the end of the one she is smoking.

"I'm not an idiot, Lisa. I know what's going on."

"Clearly, you don't."

"You and your goddamn secrets. You're becoming a bigger bitch than your mom."

The slap hits my face, and the sound bounces off the bare walls in the new house, still not completely unpacked, then vanishes like the apparition of a slap. My cheek is numb. Lisa and I stare at one another, stunned. In the twelve years we've been together, we've never once had a physical confrontation.

Lisa stares at her hand in front of her face, the hand's shadow enlarged on the wall. Slowly, she stands from her chair, her eyes cast downward. "I'm going to bed," she says in a voice just above a whisper.

I listen to her footsteps as she climbs the stairs, and then, finally, I feel the sting.

■■■

Merle Haggard wakes us at 8 a.m.—not Merle Haggard the man, rather, a recording of Merle Haggard singing "Mama Tried." We both spring up in bed.

"What the hell is that?" Lisa asks, rubbing her eyes and checking the time on her phone.

"It sounds like Merle Haggard," I say.

"Why is Merle Haggard waking us up at 8 a.m. on Saturday morning?"

"I don't know."

Lisa gets out of bed, groggy with a hangover, and walks to the window. She's wearing flannel pajama bottoms and a black tank top. I want to ravage her; instead, I swallow a Percocet while her back is turned.

"It's the goddamn rednecks," Lisa says. "They're sitting in lawn chairs outside the fucking camper, and it looks like they're already drinking beer. It's eight in the morning! I'm going to call the cops."

"What the hell are the cops going to do?"

"Grow up, Mark."

Lisa turns, and the sunlight streaming through the window catches her face. For a second, the girl in the tent is standing in the bedroom, her make-up washed off, her face soft. A face I know. Then, as quickly as it reveals itself, the sunlight slips and the face disappears, and Lisa's face is older and angry, a strange face with sharper features and a hint of the Weiss scowl. I pull a pillow over my head, hoping when I look again, the woman who made love to me in that tent in Montana will have magically returned.

But magic fails me.

"If you don't want me to call the cops then get your ass out of bed and go tell those hicks to turn their music down," Lisa says.

I stand up and grab a pair of jeans from the floor. "I don't see what the big deal is," I say under my breath.

"Will you be a goddamn man for once and not hide behind those pills?"

The statement stings, a second slap, and Lisa knows this, giving me a look that might someday mature into an apology, but I'm already bolting for the door.

As I walk out of the bedroom, I yell over my shoulder, "I bet Ron is man enough."

Three men are sitting in lawn chairs under an awning in front of the camper. The painkillers are taking hold, and as I approach the men, I'm feeling more like a marshmallow cloud than an iron tank, despite Lisa's attack on my manhood.

The man sitting in the middle chair, an incredibly large man with a good-natured gap between his front teeth, yells over the music. "You want a beer, neighbor?"

Before I can reply, he reaches in a cooler and tosses me a can of Budweiser. I lunge forward and make an improbable shoestring catch.

"Nice grab. The name's Wayne. This is my place," he says and extends his huge paw, and we shake.

"Good to meet you, Wayne. I'm Mark." Nauseous and slightly hungover, I crack open the beer. "Thanks."

Wayne turns down the music and nudges a thin guy with a baby face to his left. "This here is Jimmy," he says and nods at the other guy. "And that there is Hemi."

Hemi has a robust handlebar mustache, graying at the edges. He looks like a younger Sam Elliot in a Red Sox hat.

"I hope we didn't wake you up with the music," Jimmy says in a high, almost feminine voice. "That house has been empty for so long that we've gotten used to having these Saturday brunches without worrying about the noise."

Wayne stands from the chair, a towering figure, walks toward the side of the camper and unzips his jeans and starts to piss. "You're welcome to stick around for some food later," he calls over his shoulder. "Invite the little lady if you'd like. I'll be firing up the grill around noon."

I smile and don't say anything. After the first sip of beer, my stomach turns, churning bile, and I'm swallowing spit to keep from puking.

Meanwhile, Hemi sits there cool, quiet and handsome. There's something almost god-like about his patience, the way he watches everything without a word. But I could've sworn I saw him smirk when Wayne mentioned "the little lady." I imagine him standing below our bedroom window, waiting for me to pass out from the pills, and later sneaking upstairs where Lisa waits in the bathtub, surrounded by candles.

Wayne stops on his way back to his lawn chair then turns and lifts his hand to his forehead, shielding the sun, looking in the direction of our bedroom window. "There's the little lady," he says.

Lisa is standing at the window, her tank top clinging to her chest. I glance at Hemi, who keeps his poker-face, dragging on a cigarette.

I raise my beer to Lisa as she walks away without acknowledgement.

"Don't take this the wrong way, but she's quite a looker, neighbor," Wayne says. Jimmy nods. Hemi doesn't flinch. He knows.

Then Jimmy spits out his beer and points at the window.

We all look up like a fighter jet buzzed us overhead. Again, Lisa is at the window, only this time with her tank top lifted and her bare breasts pressed against the window. She is staring at me, her mouth fixed in the smallest of smiles. She then pulls down her top, turns and disappears.

Like magic.

The four of us stand there as quiet as the dirt below us. Finally, Hemi clears his throat. "Nice tits," he says.

I take a long pull off my beer. "I know."

The man who is fucking my wife is mythological—the god Bulfinch forgot. From a penthouse, he looks down on the plights of pathetic men everywhere; men who are anxious and dog-faced; men who are self-conscious and marble-mouthed. He watches their wives while plotting to strike with sexual lightning. A man's paranoia is his portal, his entrance into the sad bastard's psyche, and his wife's bed.

The man who is fucking my wife is elusive, a magician too slick to tip his tricks.

The man who is fucking my wife is a chameleon, blending into everyday landscapes; he is a changeling, taking on a different faces and forms.

There's no way to defend against the man who is fucking my wife. When I fall to my knees and shake a clenched fist at the sky, he laughs with a rumble of thunder. "Save it, little man," he says, "you can't fight a god with your fists."

I'm near-catatonic at the kitchen table with six empty beer bottles and a full one in front of me. I took two more pills and plan to polish off this twelve-pack.

A small crowd is gathered around a cast iron fire pit beside the camper. Someone strums an acoustic guitar, occasionally drowned by spurts of laughter or an off-key sing-along. A part of me wishes I was beside that fire, sharing a joint or a dumb joke. Instead, I watch from the kitchen of this house that is too big for the two of us.

Lisa left minutes after I returned from having beers with

Wayne and the boys. She didn't speak to me before she left. Her leaving and not returning or messaging me for eight, going on nine hours now is an affirmation of what I've known all along.

I do some quick math and try to figure out how many times a man can fuck my wife in nine hours.

The answer: too many.

The side door opens then closes. Lisa stops outside the kitchen, her shadow spreading across the tiles as wispy curls of smoke rise in indefinite directions.

"Where have you been?" I ask.

"Out."

"What was this morning all about?"

Lisa walks to the kitchen cabinet—the one she has already christened the "liquor" cabinet—and removes an unopened bottle of Smirnoff, takes out a tall glass from the dishwasher and a carton of orange juice from the fridge, and pours herself a drink. She sits down across from me, using one of my empty beer bottles as an ashtray.

"I did it for you."

"You fucked another man for me?"

"You're acting crazy. For the last time, I'm not having an affair. This is all in your head, Mark."

"You leave for the entire day after showing your tits to a bunch of strange guys, and I'm supposed to believe that I'm making this up in my head? I'm the one with the problem? You think that because I take pain medication that I'm inventing affairs?"

Lisa looks down at her glass and stirs her drink with her index finger. "How many times do I have to tell you? I'm not sleeping with anyone else. We've been living in this house for less than a week, and I already feel like I'm living alone."

I stare out the window at the fire, listening to the songs and the people's drunken laughter in the night air. It occurs to me that Lisa and I have yet to laugh, really laugh in our new house. I long to hear laughter, not slaps, bounce through these barren rooms.

Lisa stands up, walks around the table and places her hands on my shoulders. I continue to stare at the fire, but I can also see our reflections in the kitchen window, our silver wedding bands glimmering in the glass. For a moment, we're inside that tent, the thunder shaking the ground.

It's 4 a.m., and the party broke up hours ago. The cinders on the fire have nearly extinguished. Empty lawn chairs, cigarette butts, red plastic cups and beer cans are scattered around the fire pit.

Lisa looks out the kitchen window, past our reflections, where the sun is sneaking up the horizon and leaking morning light. "Let's go," she says.

The grass is wet with dew, the air cool and damp. We stand in front of the camper. Lisa tries the handle, and the door swings open. She covers her mouth, holding back a laugh.

We can make out the shapes of the objects in front of us—a dinette table bolted to the wall with cabinets above it, booth seats on both sides. A small square window looks out at our house. Lisa sits on the edge of the table and pulls me into her. I hold her head and kiss her, tasting the vodka on her tongue. She reaches for my zipper.

She spins around to face the window and lifts her skirt above her hips. She presses both palms flat on the table and glances at me over her shoulder. Before entering her, I stare out the window as the image of a tall, handsome man forms in the morning fog, grinning at me. *Now you see it.* I close my eyes and tug gently at her hair as I slide inside her. *Now you don't.*

BOULDER CITY

THEY STOOD IN A PARKING LOT outside a Mexican restaurant, one of thousands of windowless haunts off the Las Vegas Strip. With his arms around her small waist and hers wrapped around his neck, the floodlights pressed a singular shadow against the pavement. He pulled back.

"Why are you crying?" he asked.

"Because I'm never going to see you again."

"That's not true. I'll call. I'll write. I'll visit. Stop saying that." He glanced at the time on his phone. She would be waiting, sitting cross-legged on the floor of his empty apartment, a large bottle of Pinot Noir and an ashtray on the rug in front of her.

She kissed him quick, then longer, and then framed his face with her hands. "I'm never going to see you again."

"Then I'll stay."

"How can you stay? Your stuff is already packed in the truck. And what about her? What about him?"

"We'll make it work."

"You're just saying that because you're drunk."

"I'm not just saying it," he said. The shadow broke into two pieces, their heads almost touching the moon. A fat man with a goatee, carrying a Styrofoam box of leftovers, staggered past them, weaving through the cars. He waved at them, and they waved back.

"Let's get a room in Boulder City," he said. "Like we did the first night we met."

She smiled. "Imagine if the justice of the peace had answered his phone."

"I would've done it."

"Me, too," she said. "And now I'm never going to see you again."

"Then I'm staying here. With you."

"Now I know you're drunk."

"I am drunk. And I'm staying here with you." He took her small hand in his, held it steady, and mimed placing a ring on her finger. He kissed her cheek. "Say the word."

"I need to go home," she said. "He thinks I'm out with my friends."

"You are."

When he realized she was leaving, really leaving, he reached for her hand again but she had left. He found his keys and got into his car as the Las Vegas moon was muted by the lights, all of those lights. Tomorrow, he was moving back to the East Coast with a woman he hardly knew. He drove to a convenience store, played video poker for an hour, and won twenty bucks.

GLORY JEAN'S

THIS WHOLE THING HAPPENED in a period of time that I call "The Before." It was *before* the cancer took Darla; *before* Jenny vanished like a puff of smoke; *before* D.J. broke that punk's neck and got sent up to Concord for a bid where he'll probably only serve three or four years if he doesn't cause any trouble in there. It's hard to look back at "The Before" and not kick myself in the ass for not appreciating everything I had back then. But that's the slippery thing about it: *before* the shit hits the fan, we never know how good we have it. We can't know. It takes the shit hitting the fan for you to realize how much you should've appreciated the little things.

That night at Glory Jean's Tavern, our bassist Jimmy was going to sing "You Shook Me All Night Long" and that was fine with me, even though I usually sing the leads. But it would've looked downright strange seeing a guy my size try to hit some of those high notes. After tuning, I walked over to Jimmy. "You got the lyrics somewhere?"

Jimmy tapped his skull with his index finger. "They're right here, Wayne," he said.

I turned around to see if Hemi was ready at the drums, and he was twirling his sticks like he was bored and waiting for me and Jimmy to finish gabbing.

We were set up in the back of the bar, in front of the dartboards, like we were every week. Obviously, no one would throw darts while we were playing, unless they wanted the neck of my SG jammed up their ass. The place was packed, which wasn't too much of a surprise, not after Jimmy thought up a new name for our band that appeared on the sign in front of Glory Jean's. Beaming like the sun on an otherwise dark country road, the sign read: *Tonight: Free Beer and Chicken.* That was the band name Jimmy thought up—Free Beer and Chicken. He has always been clever like that.

But that wasn't the only reason for the packed house. You see, there are only three bars in Candia, and Friday night is the night everyone goes out. Glory Jean's still tends to draw an older crowd—folks, like the three of us in the band, who were in our late-thirties back then. A lot of the folks are divorced, back on the dating scene, and doing a lot of the same shit they did before they got married. A lot of them meet on dating apps now, and they are the easy ones to pick out in any crowd. They are all glossy-eyed, grinding into each other, all charged up because they aren't sick of fucking yet.

Jeff Kirby, the owner and Jean's son, had asked us to mix up our set that week—for the crowd, you know—so we added some popular songs, while still trying to stick to our blues standards. Don't get me wrong, I wasn't complaining. We got paid three hundred bucks—plus free beers—to play two sets every Friday night. For that kind of deal, I would play Air Supply's "All Out of Love"—with Jimmy singing, of course.

I gave Hemi a nod and he counted off four beats on the high hat, and I started in with the opening riff. The crowd recognized the song right away and roared their approval. The song is about sex, and there were plenty of folks aching for some sex that night. Take, for example, my ex-wife, who was standing right in front of me.

I saw her immediately with her arms wrapped around the neck of some tall, slim goon in a cowboy hat. His hands were pawing her ass like he was searching for his car keys between couch cushions. Denise was wearing a skimpy red midriff with a belly ring that gleamed like a diamond stuck in a ball of dough. Let's just say, my ex was never a small girl, even when she was using drugs, although I have to admit, she looked pretty sexy that night, like she might have lost a few pounds. Maybe she was using again. Or maybe it was the push-up bra jacking up her rack and giving the cowboy an eyeful. With his height advantage, hunched over like he was, his eyes were laser-focused on those titties.

Jimmy was singing with his eyes closed, so I doubt he saw her, but I was willing to bet that Hemi did. Denise and I had had an ugly divorce, and my buddies didn't really care for her, especially Hemi—only for different reasons. D.J., our son, still can't stand her and still hasn't spoken to her since starting his bid, refusing to see her when she shows up to visit him in prison. The only person sympathetic to Denise was Darla, who I had been married to for less than two years at that time. Darla had a heart the size of Canada, and she would always tell me that Denise was troubled and she deserved our compassion. Darla had been diagnosed with breast cancer about six months *before* and going through her first round of chemo, and she would still say stuff like that. The woman was a goddamn saint, God rest her soul.

Denise must have known I was watching her because she was really pouring it on, riding the cowboy's thigh then spinning around and rubbing her ass against his crotch. In my experiences, women generally aren't as dumb as guys when it comes to knowing when someone is looking at them. But I couldn't figure out why the hell she took this guy to Glory Jean's, where she knew my band played every Friday night, and then dry-humped him on the dance floor in front of me. I mean, Jesus Christ, she was once my fucking wife.

But that marriage was doomed while the vows were still wet

on our lips. We started dating when we were in high school, and as soon as we graduated, I started laying floors for my old man full-time. I had a steady income and a future that involved taking over the business someday, so I figured I'd marry Denise and become a family man with a house and little rug rats running around. Being a big guy, I wasn't about to take my chances on meeting someone else. I once thought that playing the guitar might get me laid, but it didn't turn out that way. Six months after exchanging rings at the city hall in Manchester, we were talking about getting a divorce. Then Denise got pregnant with D.J.

Things got better for a little while then they got worse. The breaking point came when Denise started using anything she could get her hands on. D.J. was around eight-years-old at the time, and we owned a house in Franklin. As her story goes, some guy who Denise worked with at Fed Ex was dealing all sorts of shit out of his trailer and sharing it with her, and Denise, in return, was giving up the goods. And I became a big dumb cuckold. Eventually, she moved out of the house, gave me full custody of D.J. and went and shacked up with this guy— some wiry fuck named Tom, who had this weak-ass caterpillar mustache and breath that smelled like he ate turds right out of the toilet bowl. She lived with him while we were still technically married, until Tom pulled a shotgun on her one night and chased her out. To Denise's credit, she never went back to him—not that I know of.

So I took her back, on the condition that she stop using, and she moved back with D.J. and me for awhile, but then she relapsed and was using anything she could swallow, snort or smoke, and moved out again, fucking and sucking any guy who would give her drugs. I finally filed for divorce when D.J. was still in middle school.

And there she was at Glory Jean's, lip-locked with some douche bag who was feeling her up in front of everyone while I played the soundtrack for this public performance.

If I were to tell you that my ex-wife could orgasm by having her nipples sucked, you'd probably think I was a liar. But it's the truth. Although I haven't been with a ton of women—four, to be exact—I've never been with a girl who came as easily, loudly, and often as Denise. She was like a wind-up doll. She'd come, wind-up, and come again. Believe me, it was quite the punch in the arm when we were sharing the same bed.

Darla, on the other hand, was a one-and-done girl. But after she lost her hair in that first round of chemo, we stopped having sex. I'm an asshole to bitch about it. I loved my wife—I still love her and I miss her every goddamn day—and I completely understand why she was never in the mood when she was bald with her eyebrows penciled in, throwing up and frail and perpetually whacked out on pain pills. But I still had needs. I wish I hadn't, but I did.

And it was pretty obvious that night that the cowboy was well on his way to getting his needs met. All he had to do was blow in her ear and make sure not to drink so much that he couldn't get the crane cranking. Denise was never the type of girl that you had to work all that hard to get naked. I know plenty of guys, besides myself, that have dipped their pens in that fountain. Plenty of guys.

My solo had the soul of a dead fish. I was just playing it straight from the album. I had no interest in playing songs while that cowboy son of a bitch was working his way into my ex-wife's pants. But don't start thinking that I gave a shit. The facts are that I lost my virginity to Denise, and that puts her in a special category. We were fifteen-years-old when it happened and had planned the whole thing over the telephone the night before. After hanging up with Denise, I had my older brother, Jerry, drive me to Cumberland Farms where I bought a pack of Lifestyle condoms and a bag of Cool Ranch Doritos. I kept a condom in my wallet the next day at school, taking it out during classes and holding it in the palm of my hand under the desks. I let the lubricated rubber ring slide back and forth in the packaging, itching to open it and slip it on my dick.

That afternoon, we went straight from school to her mother's apartment where we bee-lined it to Denise's cramped bedroom. She didn't seem the least bit nervous, stripping down as soon as she closed the door. She sat naked on the edge of her bed, spreading her legs and playing with herself, which caught me a little off-guard and made it pretty clear that, despite what she was telling me, it wasn't her first time. I aimed to take my pants off slow and sexy, like they do in the movies, one leg at a time, but I ended up unbuckling and yanking down my jeans like I had the shits.

The sex was quick, even with the condom. Nevertheless, it was the first time in my life that I knew, without a doubt, that I was where I wanted to be. Denise came twice, shouting to God and Jesus, and it didn't matter one lick that she'd never been to church. Afterwards, I buried my face in her hair and inhaled the scent of Pert shampoo. To this day, whenever I think of Denise, I still smell Pert.

It would be another four years, on our wedding night, until she would finally tell me what I already suspected: I wasn't her first, or her second. She'd been with three guys—one of them a forty-two year-old man—before she turned fifteen.

We finished "You Shook Me All Night Long" and I placed my guitar on its stand. Jimmy told the crowd that we were taking a short break then grabbed my arm as I tried to make for the bar to down a few beers. "What's going on, Wayne?" Jimmy asked.

"You were drifting off during that last song."

"Denise is here, and she's pretty much fucking some guy right in front us."

"Denise, your ex? I didn't notice."

"I can't see how you missed her."

Hemi came over from behind his drum set and pointed at Denise. "What's that whore doing here?" Hemi said.

While Hemi and I never talked about it, I had a good reason to believe that he put the pipe to Denise one night, and I silently hated him for it. They were flirting pretty hard after a gig we played at a biker bar in Manchester where she showed up one night, out of the blue, with some girlfriends. At that time, I had just started dating Darla, and when I left the bar that night, Denise and Hemi had ordered shots of tequila and were licking the salt off each other's wrists.

"Looks like she's getting pretty close with Cowboy Bob over there," I said.

Hemi shrugged.

Then Denise looked at the three of us and waved as she and the cowboy started to make their way over, holding hands as Denise led him through the crowd.

"Hi, boys," Denise said, standing in front of us, her arm around the cowboy's waist. "You guys sound great." She glanced at Hemi then me. She seemed pretty together, so I assumed she hadn't been popping any pain pills or snorting any smack that night, although she could have been powdering her nose with other stuff in the ladies' room.

I stared at my feet then looked up and glanced at Denise. We exchanged a look I knew too well, the look we'd give each other when we wanted to make up after a fight. Despite the fact that the woman had lied to me continuously and cheated on me many times over through twelve years of marriage; despite the fact that my wife, whom I loved to death, was sitting at home bald as a goddamn cue ball from chemo; and despite all the things that should have made me want to pretend that I had never met Denise, I couldn't help wanting to rip off her clothes and fuck her right there on the floor.

Meanwhile, the cowboy was looking around the bar like he had someplace else to be. "This is Austin," Denise said as if she just noticed he was there. She stood on her tiptoes and kissed his mouth.

The cowboy and I exchanged cold looks. I know right away when I don't like someone, and right away I didn't like that prick. I also knew it could get ugly if the cowboy didn't come to his senses and stop trying to play the tough guy by eyeballing me. It had been awhile since I'd been in a brawl at that time—and I had never gotten into one at Glory Jean's—but back in my younger days when I was still drinking the hard stuff, I had my fair share of fist fights. There are a lot of stupid men who want to take out the big guy anywhere they go. But the cowboy backed down and looked at Denise then reached around and grabbed a chunk of her ass.

"How's Darla doing?" Denise asked and tilted her head to one side, trying to look concerned. She placed her hand on my shoulder, and for that one second, when her hand was on my shoulder, I knew, if the cowboy was out of the way, I could've gone home with her. And for that one second, I knew that I would have.

"Cut the shit, Denise," I said and snarled. "You don't give a shit about Darla. Why are you here, anyway? Why don't you go someplace else?"

"Fuck you, Wayne. I ain't going nowhere," she said. "Me and Austin are dancing. Ain't that right, Austin?"

Without a word, the cowboy grabbed her hand and tugged

her back into the crowd. I had the terrible urge to go after her, cold-cock the cowboy, and take my wife back. Then I remembered that she wasn't my wife. That was *before*. Then I remembered Darla at home, her hair nuked off, wearing a fresh red bandana that she tied around her head that morning, and I felt as if I had done something so snaky and despicable to Darla that I could never forgive myself. And, in some ways, I did, and in some ways, I never have.

"What a cunt," Hemi said when Denise was gone.

He wasn't wrong.

After we packed our gear and loaded it into Hemi's van, we still had time to catch last call. The crowd had thinned, with only a handful of regulars left at the bar, all of them hoping to suck back one more round before Dean, the weekend bartender and a history teacher at a high school in Manchester, shut down the shop.

Jimmy, Hemi and I pulled up some stools, and Dean poured a Bud draft for each of us. "You sounded good tonight, boys,'" Dean said, wiping down the taps with a damp rag.

"The big guy was on fire during our second set," Jimmy said. "You would've thought Stevie Ray's spirit jumped into him." Jimmy nudged me.

It was true. The whole second set, after Denise left with the cowboy, I played from somewhere else. I lost my awareness of the crowd, and it felt like I was playing alone, trying to purge something, note by note.

It didn't work.

I turned to Hemi, who was watching highlights from the Red Sox game on the television behind the bar. "Hemi," I said, "did you ever fuck Denise?"

Hemi shot me a dirty look, his eyes pierced and nose wrinkled. "What the hell are you talking about?"

"I just want to know if you ever fucked Denise, that's all."

Stone-faced and dull-eyed, he stared straight ahead. "The bitch gave me crabs."

I sat with it for a second, letting the whole thing process. This was still *before* our friendship went to shit after he testified against D.J., although this may have been the start of it. "Was it that night we played in Manchester?"

"I came to my senses that night," Hemi said. "I saw her again at the Naswa during Bike Week."

"How was she?"

"Come on, guys. Is this necessary?" Jimmy said, shaking his head.

"You sure you want to know?" Hemi asked.

"She doesn't mean nothing to me anymore. I have Darla."

"She is a dirty girl," Hemi said in a soft voice and paused. He turned his head and looked me in the eye. "She was like the goddamn Energizer Bunny, the Energizer Bunny with crabs."

Jimmy stared into his glass like there was a message on the bottom of it that he was trying to read. I stood up and finished my beer. "I have to get home," I said and turned for the door.

Hemi stood up and stepped in front of me, placing his hand on my chest. "Wayne, don't be like that."

"Move, Hemi," I said and slapped his hand away.

"I was drunk, Wayne. Don't be mad," Hemi said, and there was something sincere in the way he said it.

I forced a smile and stepped past him. "What do I care?" I said over my shoulder. "I have Darla."

It was a quarter to two when I walked through the door. All the lights in our house were off, except for the cabinet lights above the stove. I moved through the kitchen while sticking out my arms and feeling my way through the living room into the hallway. I realized I had a little beer buzz and was a little shaky. Our bedroom door was closed, and I turned the knob and tiptoed in.

Darla was huddled in a ball on the bed with her back turned to me. Her breathing sounded like a punctured tire losing air in spurts. I could make out the shadowy shapes of the objects in the room—the lamp and the nightstand, and behind it was Darla's dressing mirror with her wig hanging on the corner. I looked at her bald head on the pillow. Quietly, I sat on the edge of the bed and kicked off my shoes. I moved my fingertips lightly over my wife's bare scalp. She stirred and placed a limp hand over mine.

"How was your gig, baby?" she asked in a sleepy voice.

"It went real good, darling. You should've heard us. We really had it tonight." I brushed her cheek with my fingers then ran them over her lips. "I was thinking about you."

"Maybe I'll make it to the next show if I feel better."

"Front row, my love," I said.

Darla chuckled then sighed. "Stop looking at my head."

"I'm not looking," I said and placed my hand back on her scalp, palming it softly and letting my fingers fall like hair. Without undressing, I lay down and put my arm around Darla. And *before* I knew it, we were asleep.

MY HUSBAND HOUDINI

RON REACHES FOR MY THIGH as my husband calls from Sacramento. A foul ball sails toward our seats then lands, ten rows back, in the right field box seats at Fenway Park.

Blasted, Mark tells me that he started drinking Mimosas at brunch and was now at a sports bar—translation: strip club—with his friend Geoff, who was recently divorced, and two of Geoff's buddies. When the crowd around us cheers for a diving catch in left field, Mark asks me where I am, his voice cracking.

"I'm at the Red Sox game with some people from work." Which isn't a complete lie. Ron is my editor at the newspaper. That much is true. However, I leave out that it is only Ron, and that what Mark has suspected for months is true: Ron is trying to sleep with me.

Maybe you're wondering what type of woman carries on a conversation with her husband, who is now becoming maudlin—Mark's telling me how much he loves me and misses me and apologizes for the way he's been acting—while another man, a man twenty years her elder, rubs her leg in an unambiguously sexual way?

The short answer, I suppose, is me.

While I'd like to think this date with Ron is platonic, it's clearly not. Meanwhile, three-thousands miles from Boston, my husband continues to fall apart.

"When I come home," he says, "I'm going to cut back on the pills and start going to AA meetings." He's slurring, his tongue turned to sludge. Music blares in the background, and I imagine a topless woman in a G-string spinning listlessly around a pole. "I'm going to do it for real this time, baby. For you. For me. For us. For real."

Ron stops a vendor selling beer, removing his hand from my thigh only to pass me a plastic cup of beer, then placing it back. I allow this.

"Mark, I have to go."

"I love you."

"Don't drive." I hang up. In March, two weeks after getting his driver's license back, Mark got a second DUI and is going to be serving three days in county jail in December. Like a stubborn child, he continues to drive drunk and whacked out on pain pills, without a license. And, quite frankly, I'm tired of mothering a grown man. I tuck the phone in my purse then place my hand on top of Ron's.

"How's your husband?"

"Drunk."

"Did I tell you how cute you look in my Red Sox hat?" he says and leans in and kisses my cheek, catching the side of my mouth.

"Ron, stop."

While I've already crossed more lines than a married woman should, the kiss in public—even if it did resemble a fatherly peck—is a step too far. Ron's been eyeing me since he came to the newspaper from *The Boston Globe*, and then tonight, after Ron picked me up at the house Mark and I recently bought, Ron said it outright. He said, "Lisa, I'm fifty years old and too old to play games, so I'm just going to say it. I don't care that you're married. I'm still interested in you."

I laughed, avoiding a response. While I'm attracted to Ron—who is handsome in a professorial way, neatly dressed with a full head of hair and salt-and-pepper beard—I don't plan on sleeping with him. Nonetheless, I'm participating in this flirting and courting, which really, if you think about it, is the type of game Ron claims to avoid, every bit of a game as the one being played in front of us. First, I accepted Ron's invitation to see a Red Sox game while my husband was away—ostensibly visiting his best friend in Sacramento, then his sister in San Jose, but it was also giving us some space to think. Now, Ron is rubbing my bare leg, and I'm not objecting. So, in a way, my response is still hovering around us, vaporous and unclear, like clouds in a crystal ball.

But here is the heartbreaking part, for me at least: Despite all of the problems in my marriage, despite the fact that my husband is a pill-popping alcoholic man-child who barely works anymore, I still love him.

The player batting for the Angels hits another foul ball in our direction, and the crowd rises to their feet. When I look up, a baseball is coming toward me. I scream and cover my head. The crowd around us then bursts into cheers and applause. Through a peephole in my fingers, I see Ron holding the baseball like a torch above his head then he bends down and hands it to me.

I blush as it seems every eye in the ballpark is focused on us. I clutch the baseball close to my chest. It's been a long time since anyone has plucked something from the air and made it mine. "That's really sweet. Thank you," I say and kiss Ron's cheek.

He played it perfectly.

While we're driving north on I-93 in his jeep, leaving Boston, he asks me if I want to go back to his place. Still holding the baseball, I tell him I've had a wonderful night, but I'd prefer to go home. He says he understands, and when we arrive at my house at one a.m., he asks if he can use the bathroom. Of course, I tell him, and he follows me inside.

The house is dark, except for the cabinet lights above the

stove, which we keep on for Gary, Mark's parrot. The bird actually belongs to his cousin Casey, a coke dealer in Manchester, who was given the bird and its cage, worth close to five-thousand dollars, as collateral from a customer who then disappeared. About a month ago, Casey was arrested during a sting, and while Casey is in jail—he couldn't post the bail, which was exorbitant—awaiting trial, Mark volunteered to take care of the parrot. So Gary, whose cage takes up a quarter of the kitchen, is ours until Casey goes to trial. While I initially didn't care for the bird—Gary was the impetus of many fights between Mark and me—I've started to warm up to him since Mark left for California a week ago.

As soon as I turn on the lights in the kitchen, Gary starts thrashing in his cage, squawking and squealing and beating his wings.

Awwk! Awwk! Fawwk you! Fawwk you!

"What the hell is that thing?"

"It's Gary, my husband's parrot. My husband thought it would be funny to try and teach it to say 'fuck you.' Don't take it personally." I place my purse on the kitchen counter and my phone starts to vibrate. "The bathroom is down the hallway, on your left."

As soon as he leaves the room, Gary stops. I grab the phone, and when Mark speaks, his voice is even thicker with booze and pills. "Hang on, baby," he says. "I'm doing my trick."

"*You* called *me.*"

"I know. Hang on."

In the background, the bar is buzzing. Then a loud male voice, which I recognize as Geoff, booms above the wet chatter, telling everyone to stop whatever they're doing and watch my husband. There is a hush followed by a female giggling.

I guess I should explain a few things. First, Mark does magic as a hobby and spends a ridiculous amount of time practicing The Disappearing Coin in front of our bedroom mirror. He has gotten good, and whenever he's drunk—which is every night now—he performs the sleight of hand trick for anyone willing to watch. Most nights, it is just me and Gary. However, Mark hasn't really bothered to learn any other tricks. In this sense, Mark's magic baffles me.

There is applause in the background mixed with a jukebox playing some kind of rock and roll. I can hear a female voice say, "That's so neat."

"Baby, they loved it," Mark says, breathless and impressed with himself.

"Why did you call?"

"I miss you."

The toilet flushes in the other room. "Call me when you're sober."

"I love you."

I hang up. As he comes out of the bathroom, I grab a bottle of Merlot from a rack below the wall clock and reach in the cupboard for two glasses. He stands in the doorway with his arms folded and his shadow splayed like a loose knot across the kitchen floor. Hysterical, Gary slams around in his cage.

"Can I interest you in a night cap?" I say.

"I was hoping you'd ask."

Fawwk you!

After two glasses of wine, it is close to two a.m. and the cigarettes come out from the junk drawer. As far as my parents and Mark know, I quit two months ago. And I have. I took up jogging and yoga and meditation, but, in a moment of weakness, I bought a pack the day Mark left and kept it in the junk drawer with some old magazines and a deck of playing cards.

After we finish the second nightcap, I refill our glasses and have a smoke. He tells me that he used to smoke but quit twenty years ago—when I was twelve years-old—and then he has a cigarette, too.

Let me say this: I like him. Despite being considerably older, as I said, I'm attracted to him, physically and intellectually. Well-respected in our profession, he carries himself as a man who knows what he wants and is not afraid to ask the tough questions. In many ways, he is Mark's antithesis. But I like him, as I said, and I enjoy his company and conversation, and as the cigarette makes me light-headed, I can see myself with him.

If I wasn't married, that is.

After our third glass of wine, we move from the kitchen to the living room couch, where he leans in and kisses me, and I kiss him back. Soon our hands are busy, rubbing and roving. Our clothes come off, and I'm on top of him in my bra and panties, sloppily kissing his face. As if sensing this, Gary goes ballistic, wailing his trained phrase again and again.

"Is there anything we can do about that bird?"

"I can cover his cage." My mouth slick with saliva, I walk into the kitchen to cover Gary's cage with a black magician's cape Mark bought for two dollars at a yard sale. When I pick up the cape, my stomach lurches, my heart hurts. This is Mark's cape, my husband Houdini's cape. As if he understands, Gary gets quiet as I drape the cape over his cage. With my head down, I go back into the living room, walking like I've been sawed in half, like I could topple at any moment.

On the couch, he is stroking himself. "Will you suck it for me?"

Like I said, he's not afraid to ask the tough questions.

I walk over to the couch and kneel in front of him and put his penis in my mouth, an act that feels as sensual as licking a stamp, but I figure I can get him off before things progress to the next step. He is really playing it up, moaning and telling me how good my mouth feels, which, if you want to know the truth, I find to be too melodramatic. Mark is a quiet lover.

Then, as he is close to orgasm, his hips quivering, he lifts my head and looks me in the eyes. "I want to be inside of you."

I've never been the type of woman to submit to a man because of pressure—in fact, I've told more than a few guys in my lifetime to go grab ice—so to say I'm coerced is simply not true. As I slide my panties down my legs and pull him on top of me, I picture the girl at the bar in Sacramento, Mark heavy-lidded and slurring, reaching behind her ear and holding a quarter pinched between his thumb and index finger, asking her if she wants to see the trick again.

The moment he enters me, I'm thinking about Mark, drunk in front of our bedroom mirror, practicing his stupid coin trick and cursing each time the quarter slips out of his hand. I try to pretend that I can't hear my phone vibrating on the kitchen table, or Gary stirring in his cage.

As he grunts and pumps, I remember the night Mark finally perfected his trick. I was in bed, scrolling through my phone, when Mark turned to me, his face beaming. "Hey babe," he said and showed me the coin, "now you see it." His magical hands moved deftly, and the coin disappeared. "Now you don't."

I clapped and smiled. "That was great, honey," I said. "You made me believe it disappeared."

THE WILD MEN

I DIDN'T WANT TO ATTEND our ten-year class reunion, but my buddy Alan, the only person from high school I still regularly talked to, had been hyping it up for months.

"We are going to do it up like the old times. We'll have a blast," Alan said in a final plea to convince me. "We'll have some drinks, spark a few."

We were having beers at The End Zone, a sports bar by the canal in Manchester, our gazes alternating between the thirty televisions tuned to games and the waitresses' asses in tight jeans as they walked past our booth.

"What if *she* shows up *with him*?"

Alan sighed. "Get over it, dude. That was a decade ago."

"But they're married now, and I'm going alone," I said.

"You're not going alone, Pudge," Alan said, smirking at me across the table. "You're going with me."

"Fuck off. And if you call me Pudge again, I'll eat your face."

I grabbed a beer from my fridge and sat down at the kitchen table in my small apartment on the third floor of an old run-down Victorian. From the window, I could see my landlord's teenage son sitting with his girlfriend in a rusted-out Toyota Corolla. Rain drizzled on the car as the two kids went at it, attempting to swallow each other's heads, their hands moving below my line of vision— reaching, fumbling, searching for something and hoping it's there.

I thought seriously about calling Alan and telling him to

forget it. While I had never been to a class reunion, I could anticipate the atmosphere: fifty or sixty of us in our late twenties dressed like we make more money than we do, bullshitting as a reflex. But I had no bullshit to bring. Ten years before, as a senior in high school, I was in a band called The Trash Gods with Alan and our friend Corky, and I was dating Rosie, the love of my life. Then in a whirlwind, everything came crashing down. Rosie dumped me, and I almost didn't graduate, and then I was arrested for drunk driving the night before graduation. Afterwards, I lost touch with Rosie. I sent her dozens of letters after she left for Cornell with her new boyfriend—now her husband—professing my undying love for her, wearing my broken heart like a badge, sending her CDs with the songs I wrote and recorded for her. But the letters went unanswered. Now, at twenty-eight, I gained some weight and was working as a paraprofessional in a middle school for slightly above the minimum wage, and Rosie taught astronomy at some small liberal arts college in New York and lived in Westchester with her husband.

Still, the thought of drinking alone in my apartment all night, while the teenage couple finger-fucked in the driveway, was more depressing than the reunion and a potential run-in with Rosie. Besides, a part of me wanted to see her again and speak to her in person, even if I had packed on some pounds since high school. Before getting in the shower, I reached into the fridge for another cold one. I was on my fourth beer. There were ten left. I counted.

Alan arrived in his company's van. He and his father were electricians and owned a small regional business with an office in Derry. He parked the van in front of my apartment and honked the horn like we were in high school again. I came out and hopped in the passenger seat. He wore a canary-yellow silk-collared shirt and pressed black slacks. Applied by the quart, his cologne could strip paint. He reached in the glove compartment and took out a joint, dropping it in my lap. "Let's take the edge off, dude," he said. "Just like high school."

I grabbed a blue plastic lighter from the console. "This shirt makes me look like I have tits," I said. I had packed on exactly twelve pounds since my last girlfriend moved out that winter, living off take-out food and pilsners.

"You look great, Pudge," Alan said. "If she shows up, she'll curse the day that she dumped you, you sexy thing."

"Don't call me Pudge."

"Did I tell you that Boner Boy is going tonight?" Alan asked, rolling down the window and allowing the breeze to run through his long wavy hair that had been his signature since high school.

"Harry Byron is going? How do you know?"

"I have my sources."

"You have your sources."

"Light the joint, dude."

"Harry Byron," I said and lit the end of the joint. "No shit."

Harry Byron grew up two streets away from me. When we were kids, I would play with Harry and this other boy Pete, who became my first best friend. It didn't take long until Pete and I ditched Harry. We were kids, and we were cruel. When Pete moved away in the sixth grade, my mom bought me a dog, a terrier-poodle mutt, to help with the loneliness. I named him Levi. One day after school, Levi bolted out of the front door and took off down the road. Gone. I searched the neighborhoods for hours, my hands cupped over my mouth, calling his name. When I walked past Harry's house, Harry came out, and without a word, helped me look for the dog. We eventually found him beside a curb, half-alive, struck by a hit-and-run driver. Harry and I carried Levi, his fur soaked in blood, back to my house, where we wrapped the dog in a wool blanket and put him in the back of my mom's car. She raced him to the vet, but it was too late. Levi was put down that night. I was devastated so I never thanked Harry for his help. Like I said, I was cruel.

In eighth grade, Alan and I became friends and started tormenting Harry for reasons I still don't understand—tripping him in the hallways and doing exaggerated impressions of his large lips, humiliating him in front of the girls. One day, Harry was called up to the front of the class to do an algebra equation on the blackboard, and like so many of us fourteen-year-old young men in the class, he had an erection. Alan and I never let him live it down, calling him "Boner Boy" straight through high school. We received no points for originality. The Trash Gods even wrote a song called "Boner Boy."

"We were assholes to that guy," I said and looked out the window of the van at a guy in a gorilla suit holding a sign for a clearance sale in a shopping plaza.

"It's Darwinian, dude. There's nothing more natural than the adolescent food chain, and Boner Boy was at the bottom," said Alan.

"That's bullshit," I said. "We were rotten."

A large yellow banner that read, *Welcome Class of '92* in bold blue letters hung above the entrance to the banquet room in a popular local restaurant. Mary Gosselin—now Mary Sandler, according to the name tag—sat behind a table collecting tickets and handing out nametags with Tricia Hart, now Lockheed. Both girls had been soccer players who ran with the popular crowd, which didn't include Alan and me, but didn't necessarily exclude us, either. We existed in a nebular space in the social hierarchy, neither here nor there. As we approached the table, the women waved in unison.

"Great to see you, guys," Mary said, grinning uncomfortably at Tricia. They had clearly forgotten our names. "I see you still have the long hair," she said to Alan.

Alan's eyes were half-shut and blazing red. He chuckled a little too loudly. "It is my hair," he said.

The three of us exchanged an awkward pause, until I finally broke the silence and pointed at the blank nametags on the table. "Elliot and Alan," I said.

Mary rolled her eyes for the histrionic effect. "I know that."

Without looking at either of us, Tricia handed us our nametags. We moved into the banquet hall where there was a cash bar to our left, a small parquet dance floor and a deejay table in the back of the room. In the dining area, round tables were covered by crisp white linen with cheap champagne bottles as the centerpieces that anchored the yellow and blue helium balloons that read *Class of '92*.

Our former classmates were huddled at the bar, standing in small and awkward social circles, essentially their same cliques from high school, half-laughing at everything.

I spotted him right away.

At the end of the bar, Harry Byron stood alone. A few pounds heavier, he had a thick, untrimmed brown beard and the same bowl-of-soup haircut, large lips and dark watery eyes.

Alan and I approached the bar and ordered beers. I tried to seem casual as I scanned the room for Rosie, but didn't see her or her husband, Blaine McMullen. I turned and stared down the bar at Harry Byron. We met eyes, and I waved. Not a facial muscle moved. There was no look of recognition. It was almost as if he didn't see me.

"Maybe this wasn't a great idea," Alan said, scratching the

back of his neck. "I don't recognize any of these people."

"So you're sure Corky isn't coming?" I asked. I hadn't spoken to Corky, the bass player for The Trash Gods, in years, not since he moved to Rhode Island where he worked as a blackjack dealer at a casino on the Connecticut border.

"When I called him, he said he would rather have his dick chopped off and served to him in a deli roll than go to the reunion."

"But you made me come to this?"

Alan shrugged. "I don't see any of the girls, either. I thought Wendy and Sherry were coming."

"So Wendy is supposed to be here?" Wendy and I dated for a little while after Rosie left for college, but the relationship didn't go anywhere, and when she moved to Portland, Maine, with a couple of friends, I stopped hearing from her. The last I'd heard she was engaged to her boss at a restaurant where she worked.

"Did you see Boner Boy over there?" Alan asked without addressing my question.

"He ignored me when I waved to him. Maybe he didn't see me," I said. Again, I turned and stared down the bar at Harry Byron and waved, making eye contact.

And, again, Harry Byron ignored me.

After the dinner, as the dessert plates, clumped with crusts of cheesecake, remained on the table, my ex-classmates got up and made their way toward the dance floor, waving their arms in the air as the deejay played House of Pain's "Jump Around."

Alan eventually caught up with Sherry, who was living in Massachusetts and working part-time as New England Patriots cheerleader. She was also engaged to a Jui-Jitsui instructor who hadn't made the trip. Alan then committed himself to sniffing her ass for the evening, ditching me despite the risk that both his legs could be snapped in half for messing with Sherry. I made my way back to the bar, alone, and saddled up with another beer.

With my back turned to the room, I felt a tap on my shoulder and turned around. There she was, looking very much the same with long dark hair and bright green eyes, and she was also very much pregnant. I looked at her with my mouth open. "Holy shit, Rosie," I said. "It's good to see you."

"It's good to see you, Elliot. You haven't changed much," she said, clearly aware that we had both put on weight, but she had a good excuse.

"I'd offer to buy you a drink, but—" I pointed at her stomach.

"I'll take a tequila shot."

"Are you serious?"

"No." She laughed. Rosie always had a good sense of humor. "How have you been?" she said and placed her hand on my shoulder. "Are you still writing songs?"

"I haven't written anything new in years," I said. This was a lie. Almost every night, I sat on the couch in my living room, fiddling with my guitar and jotting down lyrics. But the songs were uninspired and, worse yet, self-pitying. They were songs about drinking and loneliness, the search for love while feeling abandoned by it. Occasionally, Alan and I would get together and jam in the basement of his parents' house and talk about finding a new bass player and starting another band, but we never followed through with it. I kept telling myself that I was going to leave the apartment one night and play some open mics in Manchester, but I never did that, either. "Did Blaine come with you?" I asked, spitting his name through gritted teeth and a forced smile.

Rosie wasn't buying it. She tilted her head knowingly.

"It's nice of you to be concerned, but no, he is in Europe at a conference in Brussels," she said.

I nodded, punched in the gut. "I guess the two of you are doing pretty well. When is the baby due?"

"In July," Rosie said, cradling her stomach and exhaling deeply. "Listen, Elliot, I'm sorry I never wrote back to you. I got your letters, but I didn't know what to say."

"That was a long time ago," I said. "I'm over it now."

"So what are you doing now? For work, that is."

"I'm a middle school teacher. I teach music, and I'm dating one of the English teachers there," I said and sipped on my beer while thinking through my lie. "I'm probably going to pop the question soon."

Rosie smiled and nodded, as a smoke machine fired on the dance floor, and the deejay played "November Rain," which Rosie knew was unofficially our song. "That's great news, Elliot. I always knew that you'd land on your feet."

I finished the rest of my beer in a long gulp and brought the empty bottle down hard on the bar top. "Rosie, will you dance with me?"

The question seemed to stun her, and she rubbed her cheek as if she'd been slapped. After a short pause, she answered. "Thanks for the invitation, Elliot, but I better take a rain check. My feet are killing me. But it has been great seeing you," she said then turned around and, for the second time, walked out of my life, disappearing into the fog-filled dance floor.

I went outside to grab some air and stood underneath the carport in front of the entrance. There was a pair of standing ashtrays and a stone bench beside the doors. Rain fell down in sheets from edges of the canopy. Harry Byron stood with his back to me, puffing a cigarette. I stood next to him, both of us watching the rain pound the pavement. Smoke streamed out his large nostrils and dribbled from his large lips. He was an ugly man.

"Hi, Harry."

"What do you want?"

"You're not still holding a grudge from high school, are you?"

"No," Harry said, taking another drag off his cigarette. "I just don't like you."

"I can see why," I said. "I was cruel to you for a long time, and I'm sorry. And I never thanked you for helping me with my dog that day."

Harry shook his head, staring straight ahead into the parking lot. "Fuck your dog. This isn't some fucking Hollywood movie," he said. "I'm not going to forgive you and give you a big hug and then we'll share a beer. I'm not holding a grudge. I never had one. I simply don't like you. Now, leave me alone."

"Sure," I said and patted Harry softly on the shoulder then turned to go back inside.

"One more thing, Elliot," Harry called.

I stopped and turned, looking him in the eyes. "What's that, Harry?"

"You're getting fat again," he said and patted his belly.

On the dance floor, Alan was dancing with Sherry. I almost went over to tell him that I was going to call a cab and go home, but I decided against it. Instead, I went to the bar with the goal of getting wildly drunk on shots of Southern Comfort, which I could barely afford. Then, I figured, I'd track down Rosie at her table with her smart friends and tell her that I love her, beg her, one last time, to hear me out, to listen to me, to bring her pregnant self back to my place so I could light some candles in the living room and play for her the love song that I'd written for her a decade ago when I was in The Trash Gods, hoping that this time she would listen.

ALMOST CHRISTMAS

GEOFF TOLD ME OVER THE TELEPHONE that this new girl he was dating liked to be choked and slapped while getting fucked.

I said, "Geoff, this isn't going to end well."

The beer bottles were lined up, two finger-lengths apart, on the table in front of me, one plugged with wet cigarette butts. I had the phone book spread open and the number for Alcoholics Anonymous underlined in pencil. I told myself that I was going to find a meeting as soon as I got off the phone with Geoff. The next morning, I was heading to jail—doing three days in county after my second DUI. Something like a clenched fist had been floating in the center of my chest for weeks, a hardened pit of fear. I'd never been to jail and never imagined I would. I'm soft. And somewhere, at that very moment, my estranged wife was probably fucking her new boyfriend, straddling him in the same bed where we once slept. And somewhere, Geoff's ex-wife was probably fucking this cop she was seeing while Geoff was talking to me about his new girl, a divorcee who worked at a Target in Sacramento and liked to be roughed up. And somewhere, even farther away, there was this vague recollection, the dimmest of the dim stars, that all of this, at one time, used to be fun.

A beer popped on the other end of the line. "The other morning, when I was coming out of the shower," Geoff paused and sipped and burped. "And Mark, I'm not shitting you, my friend. Cindy was standing in front of my bedroom mirror in her bra and panties, talking to herself in a baby voice. Then she turned to me and asked, in this baby-voice, if I'd choke her."

"Did you?"

"I couldn't."

It was almost Christmas, and the convenience store across the street had recently put a single plastic candle behind the bars in the front window. It hummed to me. "Geoff, you're a good man."

"No, I'm not," he said, and kept drinking.

Part III

THE NEXT STEP

ANNIE'S HAIR SMELLED OF CIGARETTES, a fruity shampoo and the earthy scent of scalp. "What's the worst thing that you did when you were using?" I asked her.

"You don't want to know."

"What does it matter? It's in the past."

Annie ran her nails through my hair, which seemed to be thinning. "You really want to know?"

"I want to know."

She rolled on her side with her back to me and faced the bedroom window, looking at the four-way intersection outside my apartment. In the kitchen, my parrot Gary was stirring in his cage. "When I was waiting tables in my twenties, I went to a party one night with some coworkers, and we had a gang bang."

"Oh." It was all I could say. "Was it all guys?"

"I told you that you didn't want to know."

"It's all right," I said, finding my voice. "I had a wild side, too." I reached for my cigarettes on the floor beside the full-sized mattress that I bought on liquidation after moving out of my house. My wife had taken the bed and the solid oak frame, along with the house and most of the dignity I was trying to reclaim. That was one of the reasons that I started attending AA—along with a court mandate that followed a three-day stint in jail and a seven-day stay in a program for recidivist offenders. That was eight-nine days ago. Like a sculptor chipping away at a stone, I was trying to carve a stronger, sober, solid man out of the amorphous mess I had become. But sometimes, truth be told, I missed the amorphous me, the guy without dignity or definition. I couldn't tell you why I missed him, but I did.

Outside my apartment, a car slammed its brakes and a horn blared at the intersection. Since I had moved into that one-bedroom on the West Side of Manchester—one of the only places that would allow me to keep Gary—there had already been three accidents at that intersection. Annie stood and draped a sheet around her chest, picking up her bra and panties from the clothing scattered like confetti on the dusty bedroom floor.

"Where are you going?"

"I should leave," she said, her back turned as she started to dress. "Sharon warned me about getting into relationships during the first year, especially with someone from the program. I feel like I want a drink now."

"Do you want to get one?"

"I hope you're joking," she said, her eyes narrowing. "You're getting your green chip tomorrow."

I grabbed my two-month gold chip from the small nightstand—some of the only furniture I managed to get in the separation—and held it up in front of me. "Watch this, Annie," I said and showed her the chip. "Now you see it." I moved my other hand in front of it and performed a sleight of hand, showing her my empty palms. "And now you don't."

"That's not funny," she said.

"I'm sorry." Sweaty and naked, I grabbed a pair of boxer shorts from the floor and put them on. "Annie, don't leave. I don't care about your past. It just caught me off-guard."

Annie lit a cigarette, took a couple of drags then flicked the ash into the mouth of a Diet Coke can. "I can't pretend those mistakes never happened and, to be honest, I feel like I'm making another one now."

She was a thin woman, and I held her boney hand in mine. "Listen, I've really enjoyed being around you, and I don't care what our sponsors say." I had yet to tell Rick, my sponsor in the program, about Annie, who I had slept with twice, including the night before. "Besides, I don't care what it says in The Big Book. You're helping me stay sober."

Another car laid on its horn at the intersection. Annie pulled her hand away, bent down and pecked me on the cheek. "I have to be at work in a few hours."

I tried pulling her back into bed. "Don't leave. We can go out for breakfast," I said. "I'm really nervous about having to talk at the meeting tomorrow night. I could use someone to talk to."

"Call your sponsor," Annie said and flipped her hair off her shoulders, a sassy and delicate gesture that seemed to punctuate something, then pulled it back into a ponytail. Annie had been sober for two months longer than me, and she already told her story of experience, strength and hope when she received her green ninety-day chip. "You're going to be fine. At least you never participated in a gang bang," she said, reaching for her keys in her purse.

"Who said I didn't?"

"Very funny."

"Breakfast?"

"Not today."

"Will you call me later?"

"I'll try." And with that, Annie was gone, out the door, and gone. I had the distinct sense that she had just broken it off with me. My old self—the amorphous me—surfaced without a day of sobriety and followed Annie out the door, turned left at the convenience store with the bars in its window, walked down the street to Rocky's Pub and ordered a Bloody Mary then scored some brown dope from Julius in the apartment upstairs. He then called his doctor, explaining that the excruciating back pain he had since a car accident in his early-twenties had returned, tenfold, and begged him for a new script.

I lit a cigarette, a habit that I started when I moved out of the house and had exacerbated when I got sober and needed something to compensate for the vices that I quit. I watched the cars crawl toward the intersection, stop for a blink then ease forward.

I stepped onto the hiking trail in an old pair of Nikes, beige cargo shorts and a Coors Light t-shirt that I picked up at some bar promotion years ago. Ten yards ahead of me, Rick looked like he had been clipped from a J-Crew catalogue—expensive hiking boots, a thin fleece vest, a sweat proof t-shirt, socks made of some fabric designed to prevent blistering, and a sleek forest green pack strapped to his back. Nearly a decade before, when Rick arrived at his first AA meeting, he was a rock-bottom gutter drunk, and like many recovering alcoholics, he replaced his drinking with a healthier obsession for exercise, chiseling his alcohol-ravished body into a picture of fitness. Rick had been begging me to hike with him since becoming my sponsor two months ago. As a fairly new cigarette smoker, the thought of walking up a mountain didn't exactly appeal to me, but after Annie left that morning, I knew it wouldn't do much good to mope inside the apartment all day, thinking about drinking and scoring dope. So when I called Rick that morning to chat, before I could get a word in, he asked me if I wanted to climb Mount Tecumseh, and I foolishly agreed.

I was short of breath a quarter of a mile up the trail, feeling the cigarettes in my chest. "How long is this going to take?" I asked.

"It's only about an hour and a half to the top."

"Three hours total?"

"You'll live," he said.

I brushed a branch from my face. "I met a girl, Rick."

He stopped on the trail and turned to me. "You know what I'm going to tell you."

"She's in the program."

"That's worse. You'll end up enabling each other. I've seen it happen too many times, Mark. You need to focus on your sobriety, and not mess around with new relationships right now. Concentrate on your relationship with booze and drugs."

"So I can't get laid, either?"

Rick sighed and started back up the mountain. "If you stay sober through the first year, you'll have the rest of your life to get laid, my friend. But you're fighting for that life right now and putting yourself in a very dangerous position."

"This whole thing sucks," I said like a defiant child.

"Sometimes sobriety sucks. But it beats the alternative."

We then walked into a small grove, and the sun poked out momentarily behind a gathering of dark clouds hovering above the distant mountains. The air was thick and humid, and I noticed the sweat drenching my t-shirt. *Fuck this*, I thought, glancing at the sky. *Fuck all of this.*

The rain moved in and was pounding the rock face as we climbed out of the woods and I stared up at a towering crag. Rick removed a poncho from his pack and tossed it to me. "I didn't think you'd remember one," he said.

"We're not really going to climb to the top, are we?"

"You don't have to come," he said as he pulled a second poncho over his head. "I'll meet you back here in twenty minutes."

I reached in the pocket of my cargo shorts for my cigarettes and a lighter. "Can you toss me the keys? I'm going to head back down and wait in the car." And I'd have to wait in the car. My driver's license was still suspended and would be for quite some time.

Rick lobbed me the keys, which landed on a rock with a thunk. "I'll see you in a couple of hours," he said and started up toward the summit.

Pissed off with a cigarette lit dangling from my lips, I turned and headed into the woods, back down the trail. As the rain continued to fall in sheets, I had a moment of displacement, a moment where I became lost in the context of my own life. I couldn't understand how I had ended up here, sober as a stone, hiking a mountain. I thought about my father, a functional drunk all his life—and a fucking asshole—and what he might think if he saw me now, if he were still alive. I couldn't understand how it was Annie, and not my estranged wife Lisa, who slept in my bed the previous night. And I couldn't understand why, in God's name, I was preparing to spill my life's story to a room of relative strangers the next night. The only thing that seemed remotely familiar, the only part I understood, was the desire pounding inside of me to have a drink and get high.

Then I slipped on a wet stick and started falling—tumbling and tearing, out of control, down the trail.

When I heard the snap, I wasn't sure if it was a stick or my neck or another bone in my body. I came to an abrupt stop against a birch tree and lay like a slab of steak, motionless. I stared at the swirling storm clouds above me, the rain pounding my face, and wiggled my hands and my toes. I hadn't broken my neck, but a hot pain pulsed in my right leg, and when I glanced down, I saw a bone protruding from my ankle, poking out from my white sock, which was already soaked in blood. Nauseous and dizzy, I threw back my head and screamed for help.

■■■

It felt like hours that I sat on the trail in agony, waiting for Rick—or any hiker—to arrive and help me, and I had no phone service on the mountain.

In actuality, it was only about ten minutes until Rick arrived. I was unable to put any weight on my foot so I hopped, gingerly, with my arm around Rick's shoulder, down the mountain until we reached the trailhead then drove directly to the emergency room in Plymouth. It was the most pain I had experienced since the car accident where I fractured a vertebra.

The rest of the afternoon passed in a blur, largely due to the pain medication that was administered, which I legitimately needed for a change. There were x-rays and doctors and nurses and the unforgiving brightness of the hospital lights. Eventually, I dozed off on a gurney covered by a crisp linen sheet, riding a glorious pharmaceutical cloud. When I woke, Rick was sitting beside me in a padded chair, thumbing through a fitness magazine. "What's going on?" I asked him, running my tongue—dry and heavy—over my gums.

"You broke your ankle," Rick said. "The good news is that the doctor who set it said he doesn't think you'll need surgery, but he wants you to see a specialist in Manchester, just in case."

"I'm on a lot of drugs."

"They said the pain and inflammation will be severe for a few days. They're going to give you some medication to get you through until you see the orthopedist."

"Does that mean I lost my sobriety?"

"We're not all purists, Mark. If you're in pain, you should treat the pain, but you need to get off the pills as soon as you can, especially with your history. I've seen this kind of thing lead to a relapse. It's tricky because only you know that line when taking them for pain crosses into something else."

"I guess I'm not cut out for hiking," I said.

Rick laughed. "Something occurred to me as I was helping you down the trail," Rick said. "If we had been drinking," he pursed his lips and closed his eyes. "If we had been drinking, you'd probably still be on that mountain."

"If we had been drinking, we would've been at a bar, and not on top of that stupid mountain," I slurred.

Rick sighed. "Go easy on the painkillers, cowboy," he said, thwacking the side of the bed with his curled magazine.

We left the hospital with enough drugs to get me through until Monday morning when I had an appointment with the orthopedist in Manchester. The doctor, a lanky intern with an enormous Adam's apple, told me I wouldn't be able to drive with my right foot in a cast. I laughed and nodded and told him it wasn't an issue.

Rick helped me up the stairs to my apartment, and I set up camp in the living room, in front of the television, with my leg elevated on a stack of pillows and my metal crutches on the floor beside the couch.

"If you need anything, give me a call," Rick said and ruffled my hair. "Are you sure you don't want me to stay the night?"

"Unless you can take a leak for me, I'm not sure you can help with anything else."

"In my drinking days, I would keep an empty plastic jug beside my bed before I passed out so I wouldn't have to get up to piss in the middle of night. If you have an empty jug, it might save you a few trips."

I shook my head. "I think I'll be all right," I said and extended my hand. "Thank you, Rick."

"Good luck," he said and shook my hand. "I'll call you tomorrow morning. We'll see how you're feeling and if you're up for speaking at the meeting tomorrow night."

"It's my ninety-day chip," I said. "I don't want to miss that meeting."

"I'm proud of you, Mark," Rick said. "You're doing one of the hardest things a person can do. Remember that."

"I appreciate you," I said.

Then Rick left, and the second the apartment door shut, I hoisted my body up on my crutches and gimped down the steps, out of my apartment and onto the sidewalk. I hobbled to the convenience store across the street where I bought two bottles of cheap white wine and proceeded to get shit-faced.

With the wine buzz amplified by the painkillers, on top of a severely compromised tolerance, I called Annie at two a.m. I was still planning to speak about my experience, strength and hope at the meeting at St. Anthony's that night and wanted to practice my speech with her.

She picked up. "Is something wrong? Why are you calling this late?"

"I'm celebrating the ninety most miserable fucking days of my life."

"Oh Mark."

"I broke my ankle on a stupid hike," I said.

"How much have you had to drink?"

With my leg elevated and the second bottle of wine nearly empty, I looked out on the intersection and the four stop signs. "Why don't you come over? We can talk about it."

"You need to call your sponsor," said Annie.

"I'll see you tomorrow night, I mean, tonight, right? Look I rhymed," I said, laughing at my own joke. "You and me, baby. Let's have some friends over and have a gang bang."

"Fuck you, and call your sponsor."

She hung up, and I stared at my phone as the television splashed bluish light throughout the living room. I was a fucking asshole. I thought about calling Rick, but then my cigarette fell from my fingers and burned a small hole in the carpet.

We arrived early at the basement of St. Anthony's church so Rick and Bruce—a burly biker and an old-timer in the program—could set up the folding chairs and put on the coffee urn. As the secretary for The Happy Hour West meetings at St. Anthony's, I usually helped set up the room, but due to my ankle, Rick and Bruce gave me a pass that night. When Bruce asked me what happened, I told him the boiled-down to the essentials version of the story I would tell people for the rest of the night: I fell, and it was Rick's fault.

However, I hadn't told Rick about falling off the wagon, but I had a vicious hangover that even the Percocet couldn't touch. I had almost forgotten the tick-tock torture of the hangover. By the time Rick picked me up, I had rallied enough to hide the empty bottles beneath the sink and I tried to sponge-bathe the stink of booze from my skin and covered it up with cologne. From the second he arrived, Rick's enthusiasm made it difficult to slip in the fact that I was a fraud.

As the room began to fill with the first-name faces of recovering drunks and drug addicts, I sat in a pharmaceutical stupor behind a table in the front of the room, my leg elevated on a chair with a throw pillow Rick grabbed from the rectory. Behind me hung a banner with felt lettering that read *Keep It Simple*, and Rick stood at the solid wooden podium to my left, looking through his meeting notes. It occurred to me that I should leave, and I was contemplating grabbing my crutches and hobbling to the exit without another word, back to my old life and the amorphous me, when I noticed Annie standing in front of me.

"Congratulations," she said in a voice as flat as a skipping stone. Before I could respond, she had turned her back and sat down in the front row beside a woman with frizzy red hair and an overbite, a woman named Sharon who Annie once introduced to me as her sponsor.

When Rick pounded the gavel on the podium and called the meeting to order, I had nowhere to run. The only options were to tell the truth, to come clean to the members of Happy Hour West when I was called to share my story and use my sleight of hand trick on my ninety-day chip as well, then sit back down, salvaging a shred of the dignity that I had vowed to reclaim. Or I could stand in front of the room on my crutches and lie like an addict.

I kept my eyes downcast as Rick read the announcements— the week's calendar and commitments. When I looked up during "The Serenity Prayer," Annie was staring at me, frowning.

Rick then handed out the chips to the people in the room celebrating their sobriety dates, withholding mine. When he was finished, Rick paused, nodded to me and reached into the chip tray for my green chip.

"I not only have the pleasure of introducing tonight's speaker, but also have the pleasure of being his sponsor, and I'm also largely responsible for the cast you see on his leg," Rick told the room.

The crowd laughed as Rick told the story about our hike, my bitching on the way up the trail, then quitting before reaching the top. They nodded their heads as he told them about his epiphany, the one he shared with me in the hospital room, which he now called a metaphor for the process of sobriety. "If it weren't for the grace of God keeping us sober, Mark might not be here tonight to share with us." Rick paused again and patted my back. "I can't tell you how proud it makes me to give Mark his chip for three months of sobriety. You've has earned this, buddy. Mark, my friend, congratulations."

The crowd stood up from their seats and applauded. As I propped myself up on my crutches and made my way to the podium, Annie glared at me, stone-faced and slow clapping. As Rick handed me my ninety-day chip, the amorphous me emerged, and I sensed that I was about to do something much worse than anything I'd ever done, wasted or sober, in my life.

BIRTHDAY AT THE HIBACHI BAR

THE HIBACHI CHEF BALANCES a green pepper on the end of a spatula. There's a metallic clank as he claps it with a second spatula and the pepper arcs through the air and lands effortlessly in Stephanie's mouth. The hibachi chef bows.

"That's amazing," Stephanie says, brushing against my arm. "I wish I could do something amazing like that."

"I read somewhere that they bring some of these chefs over from Japan on work visas. Most of them work for a year then return home," I say and fill our small ceramic cups with warm sake. In the dim lighting, you would never guess that I'm decades older than Stephanie. Last semester, she was one of my composition students at the community college, a fact that still shames me. Two months ago, the day after my divorce was finalized, I saw her at a bar where I was drowning my sorrows, and we started talking. Then flirting. Then touching. Then we went back to my small studio apartment. We've seen each other almost every night since. We've only been out in public a few times—once to a bookstore and once for a pizza, and now here at the hibachi bar. Our waitress at the pizza place asked if she was my daughter, and we blushed and tried to laugh it off, but it was obvious that it deeply embarrassed both of us. We told her that we were just good friends.

Tomorrow, I turn forty-three and will spend the day with my sixteen-year-old son, who is closer to Stephanie's age than me—they listen to the same music and share the same pop-culture referencing, quoting lines from *SpongeBob SquarePants* to each other the one time they met.

My colleagues and my ex-wife believe Stephanie is a part of my midlife crisis, but I disagree. While Stephanie and I have had more sex in the past month than I had in the last ten years of my marriage, it is more than just physical. I like Stephanie. She's a great conversationalist, witty and wry, and I love the way she laughs, covering her mouth with her fingers and squealing slightly. Although I'm still unsure what a girl so young and pretty would see in me, a middle-aged divorced man with a beer paunch and an adolescent son. Tonight, Stephanie is celebrating my birthday with me.

She raises the cup and slams back the sake then faces me and takes a deep breath. "There's something we need to talk about." She stares at her fingernails, long and lacquered and red.

"You're not breaking up with me, are you?"

"I'm not breaking up with you," Stephanie says and tucks a strand of silky brown hair behind her ear. "But I need to tell you something."

I place my hand on her forearm. "Is it bad?"

"It's not good," she mumbles, still staring at her hands.

The hibachi chef scoops the rice for the stir fry onto the flattop grill and mixes in the vegetables, clanking out a steady, martial beat with the spatulas.

"It can't be that bad," I tell Stephanie.

"I did a porno," she says in one unpunctuated breath.

"What?" I turn my ear toward her mouth, making sure I heard her correctly.

"I did a porno film when I was eighteen, and I wanted you to hear it from me first in case you hear it from someone else, like my ex-boyfriend."

"Do you mean to tell me you're a porn star?"

"I'm not a porn star," she says. "It was just one video. I was desperate for cash and I answered an ad online to do some modeling. The guy who placed it, some rich guy from Nashua, told me I would only have to pose nude and that the pictures were for a private collection. He told me no one would see it and he offered me a lot of money. My parents had kicked me out of the house, and I really needed the cash. And once I was there, he offered me more money to give him oral on camera. It was a lot of money. It paid my rent for three months."

I shake my head as the spatula's backbeat quickens, building to a crescendo..

"I was doing a lot of coke in those days, but that's not an excuse."

"Can I watch it?"

Her eyes grow wide with horror, her hands balled into tight fists, nails tucked. "Why on earth would you want to watch it? I thought you respected me."

"I do," I say and suddenly I have this horrific image of my sixteen year-old son watching a clip of my girlfriend giving head to the disembodied cock of a man whose face will never appear.

The hibachi chef holds up a plastic squirt gun and yells, "Sake, birthday boy." I open my mouth and he fills it with the lukewarm rice wine. I try to swallow it without choking, but I spit up like an infant on the front of my shirt. Ashamed, I turn to Stephanie and shrug, but she will no longer look at me.

An Evening with Dr. Terrific

LAUREN'S LAWYER IS A STERN and humorless woman with sharp shoulder blades and long silver hair pulled into a tight bun. She sits behind an oak desk, staring at her phone with her reading glasses resting on the bridge of a long thin nose.

I'm sitting across from her in one of the two black leather chairs in a small office in Concord, waiting for my wife and staring out the window at a Volkswagen spinning its back wheels in the snowy parking lot and trying not to scratch my crotch. While the rash has healed considerably over the weekend, the heavy silence in the office is making me hyperconscious of its remains.

"Would you like a bottle of water?" Lauren's lawyer asks. Her name is Sadie Lutz, and it's fairly clear that she doesn't care for the male species and would've delighted in making minced meat of me if this had gone to court.

"Do you have a beer?"

"I don't stock alcohol in the office."

"I was joking."

She finally peers up from the phone screen, meeting my eyes. "I've read the divorce papers, sir. I tend to doubt that it was a joke."

Lauren should be arriving any minute, and we're slated to sign the papers before a judge puts the whole matter to rest, but I'm still hoping that all of this can be avoided with an eleventh hour miracle, my final Hail Mary. After this past weekend, I'm still hoping that Lauren and I will realize that there is a love worth saving here, tear up the divorce papers, and salvage our marriage.

I'm still trying not to scratch.

The rash started on Thursday night while I was lounging alone in my apartment, watching *Law and Order* and reheating some leftover pizza. It started as a quick itch, a mild discomfort—nothing earth-shattering. Then, as I parked myself on the couch to eat in front of the television, my crotch started to tingle. By the end of the show, the itch became more aggressive, the scratching so frenetic that my hand became a rake.

Later, I was in bed running through the list of worrisome questions that keep me awake most nights. When can I quit my tedious job as a paraprofessional at a high school and find something fulfilling to do with my life, even as I close in on fifty-years-old? What would I find fulfilling? How am I going to pay my divorce lawyer? Why don't I pick up my guitar again and start a new band? Or why don't I call Alan and revive The Trash Gods? Why don't I renew my gym membership to address my fat ass and the twenty pounds I've gained in the past year since moving out of the house? That was when the itching became persistent and the rash had expanded down my inner thigh. By midnight, after swallowing a couple of Benadryl, it had become a red-alert case of crotch-rot.

I barely slept the rest of the night as I scratched, trying to figure out the cause of the rash. It wasn't jock itch. It was January, in the middle of an Arctic blast, and I hadn't broken a sweat in more than a month. It wasn't an STD, seeing I hadn't been intimate with anyone since moving out of the house. Eventually, I quit trying to sleep and went to the internet to find a diagnosis. That was a bad idea. After searching on Google, I discovered it could be anything from an innocuous fungus to a life-threatening staph infection. And looking at the pictures online was like watching a snuff film. There are few things worse than itching and scratching without an explanation or a means of relief. I suppose it's safe to assume that being water-boarded, garroted, drowned, or anything that involves suffocation is worse, but the inexplicable itch holds a solid place on that list.

Also making the list is agreeing to go to dinner with my soon-to-be ex-wife and my sixteen-year-old daughter the next night at the house where I once lived to meet my wife's new boyfriend, Dr. Terrific—an associate English professor at the University of New Hampshire who has recently published his third novel.

And did I mention that I've gained twenty pounds?

The next morning, I slathered Cortisone cream on my crotch in the faculty bathroom between classes. I assist a special education teacher in her supported study courses, helping the students with IEPs or learning disabilities with whatever work they've been assigned in their academic classes, and I was moving around the classroom that day like a mouse on methamphetamines to keep from scratching my crotch.

But I muscled through the school day instead of calling in sick and went home and swallowed more Benadryl—it didn't even introduce the concept of drowsiness the previous night, but then I felt like I needed a nap—and while getting dressed for dinner with Dr. Terrific, I also came to terms with the fact that I either needed to lose weight or buy new pants. When I was younger, I was a chubby kid, and my parents used to call me Pudge, which they thought was cute and funny. It wasn't. My whole life I've fluctuated between pudgy and trim. But now at forty-eight years old, it's getting harder and harder to lose weight. I could probably deal with the weight gain and buying new pants, but when you add having to meet my wife's new boyfriend, and the itching on top of everything else, it seemed like a reasonable time to lay down and die.

On the way to Lauren's house—I almost said "our" house—I stopped at CVS for a bottle of wine and another tube of Cortisone cream. I picked out a bottle of Sutter Homes chardonnay. After fifteen years of marriage, I know that Lauren likes Sutter Homes wine, and after a string of years making her miserable, I wanted to make her happy. I knew the chances of reconciliation were slim, seeing our divorce was going to be finalized in three days and she had a new boyfriend, but I still held onto the faintest of hopes that we'd recall what initially brought us together back when we met at a gig one night in Londonderry, when I was still playing in a band and not carrying around the extra twenty pounds. I started talking to her at the bar between sets, gave her my number and promised to play The Replacements "Kiss Me on the Bus" for her during our second set. That sealed the deal. We kissed in the parking lot outside her car that night, and the rest took care of itself. While neither of us ever stepped out on our marriage when we were living together, we stopped working at it, or paying attention to each other, and the passion faded and, eventually, we stopped kissing altogether.

While waiting in a line at the drugstore, I focused on the soft music piping in from the ceiling—Asia's "Heat of the Moment"—and found myself choking up, thinking about Lauren. To keep from crying—I've cried enough privately—I focused on playing the solo on the air guitar, and for a second, I forgot about the itching.

"You're next, Mr. D.," a voice called, snapping me out of my solo. It was Matt Wagner, a student in the fourth period supported study who was working the cash register.

Bull-legged, I walked toward the check-out and placed the bottle of wine and tube of Cortisone cream on the counter. I smiled at Matt. "How is it going, Matt?"

"Not so good, Mr. D.," he said and scanned the bottle, frowning.

"I'm sorry to hear that," I said, hoping the conversation would stop there. Matt is a good kid, but I had my fill of bad news by that point.

Unprompted, he said, "My girlfriend dumped me, and now she's chillin' with some other dude and just posted a picture on Instagram of them together in her bedroom. It was only twenty minutes ago, and already has a shit-ton of 'likes'."

"I'm really sorry to hear that, Matt," I said. I wanted to tell him to look at this as a dress rehearsal for a divorce when he becomes an adult, only the divorce will be messier and more expensive and, emotionally, it will feel like your heart was ripped out of your chest, still beating, and handed to you on a plastic dish. "Maybe they're just friends."

Matt looked at me like I had hummingbirds flying out of my ears. "I doubt that," he said. "That'll be $21.97."

I swiped my card then waited for the receipt to print, enshrined in a long pause. "I'm getting divorced on Monday," I said for some inexplicable reason.

Matt ripped the receipt from the machine. "I'm sorry, Mr. D. Does it ever get any easier?" he asked and paused, his eyes wide awaiting my response.

I grabbed the wine and the receipt. "I'll let you know," I said and fought the urge to scratch as I walked through the automatic doors and into the bone-cold night.

I went on a low-carb diet three months before my wedding. While my breath smelled like shit as I gouged myself on protein, and I would've stabbed my own mother for a slice of cheese pizza, it worked. Within two weeks, I dropped eleven pounds, and after a month and a half, I was looking svelte, which after years of battling weight fluctuation, increased my energy and confidence and sex-drive. Lauren and I were having sex just about every night when we were first married and Haley was still sleeping in her crib. But then I started to cheat on the diet—a beer here, a slice of pizza there. The next thing I knew I had reintroduced the loaded steak and cheese, beer and nachos.

That was the end of that.

The weight came back in a tsunami. When the whole process was said and done, I had actually gained five pounds from when I started. Now I'm fifteen pounds heavier than that, which was twenty pounds heavier than I was when I first married Lauren. My weight has become a math problem. And there I was, standing under the porch light of the home I once owned with Lauren—where we raised our daughter—holding a bottle of white wine and waiting for the woman I love to answer the door. The whole situation would make a great set-up for a break-up song, if I were still writing songs. I might call it "White Wine with a Side of Pride".

When Lauren answered the door, I stopped myself before groaning like I'd been kicked in the groin, which was how it felt. For the last two years we were married, Lauren seldom wore earrings or dresses or makeup. If we went to dinner—which wasn't often—she might put on some light mascara and lip gloss and change into a skirt or designer jeans, but I hadn't seen the woman standing in the door frame for almost three years. Her dirty-blonde hair was clipped back, silver hoops dangled from her earlobes, her lipstick glittering in the porch light. I began to itch.

"Come in, Elliot," she said and stepped aside, not meeting my eyes—like she knew. "I'll try to make this as painless as possible," she whispered as I took off my jacket and placed it on the wooden coat rack beside the door.

"You look great," I said, following her through the kitchen.

She glanced over her shoulder and smiled crookedly. "Thanks."

The whole point of the dinner that night was to model for our daughter the way reasonable adults can remain friendly and respectful, despite their differences. We wanted to show Haley that sometimes you need to swallow your pride in the name of kindness. Haley has struggled with the separation, her grades fell and she has had some uncharacteristic discipline issues in class, and both Lauren and I agreed that we should play nice, for Haley's sake. However, the addition of Dr. Terrific's presence at the dinner table that night had caught me off-guard, but I decided I would bite my tongue, for the sake of harmony.

I followed Lauren into the kitchen where a prime rib was roasting in the oven. The furniture was essentially the same stuff we had when I lived there—the island, the oak dinner table and four matching chairs—but there were now two new wooden barstools facing each other at the end of the island and an empty wine glass in front of each. Lauren works for Fidelity Insurance, handling investments portfolios, and makes four times my salary, including my summer job painting houses. I handed Lauren the bottle of Sutter Homes, and she glanced at it and pushed out her bottom lip. "You remembered," she said.

"It's your favorite," I said, pressing my knees together and holding my breath, trying not to scratch my crotch.

"Is something wrong, Elliot?"

"I have a thing," I said. "It's a rash, and it itches like a son of a bitch."

"There is some Cortisone cream upstairs."

"I brought my own."

Lauren placed the wine in the refrigerator and grabbed a bottle of Bud Light for me. From where I was standing, I glimpsed in the fridge and saw a single six-pack of Bud Light surrounded by dark bottles of craft beer. "Are you still drinking every night?" Lauren asked me.

"This is the first beer I've had all week," I said, which was mostly the truth. I had a few in the lounge while waiting for a pizza on Tuesday night, but otherwise, I had been trying to stay relatively sober.

"It was getting a little out of hand."

"I know," I said. My drinking had contributed largely, not only to my weight game, but the dissolution of my marriage. When we were married, I had spent far too many nights playing shows, or watching shows, in bars and clubs around the city, and not nearly enough time at home with my wife and daughter.

"Haley and Ryan are in the dining room," Lauren said, leading me into the same room where I once shared nightly meals with her and Haley, who was barely acknowledging me as a human being, much less her father anymore. Looking more and more like her mother these days—the same thin frame and long legs, straight blond hair and full mouth—Haley was sitting at the dining room table staring at her phone. She didn't look up when I entered the room.

Across from her, a youthful-looking man in his early-forties, slight with a closely clipped beard and Hollywood blue eyes, stood and extended his hand. He had the daintiest hands I have ever seen on a man. I have large hands with long fingers and calluses on the tips from playing the guitar, and for some reason, my hand dwarfing his hand felt like a victory. "I'm Ryan," said Dr. Terrific. "It's good to finally meet you."

"It's terrific to meet you," I said, releasing his tiny paw then sitting at the end of the table, across from Lauren. I nodded to my daughter, who still hadn't looked up from the phone. "Hi, sweetie," I said.

"Hello father," Haley said in a monotone.

The itching hit me like a gunshot, and my crotch caught fire. I sprung up from my chair, nearly spilling my beer. "I need to use the bathroom," I said and hustled out of the dining room, past the guest bathroom by the front door, and up the hardwood stairs to the second floor. I flipped on the bathroom light and slammed the door behind me.

The bathroom looked the same—the same lavender shower curtain, the same lavender floor mats, the same vanity and medicine cabinet above the sink. I took the Cortisone cream from my pocket and dropped my pants. With my right palm open, I opened the cap with my teeth and squeezed a quarter of the tube into my hand, slathering it on myself. I sat down on the toilet with my pants around my ankles and waited for the itching to subside. That's when I spotted the beard clippers on the bathroom counter beside the sink. I sighed and tried to gather myself.

When I returned to the dining room, the three of them were huddled toward Lauren's end of the table. As soon as I sat down, Lauren sat up, straight-backed, her hands folded in front of her. "Is everything all right?" she asked.

"It's fine."

Lauren nodded and stared at her lap as Dr. Terrific reached across the table and placed his itsy-bitsy little hand on Lauren's forearm. "Lauren tells me you're a musician," he said. "I tried to learn the guitar in college, but I have terrible rhythm."

I tried to picture those tiny hands stretching across a fretboard to play one of those difficult jazz chords. Impossible.

"I hear you have your own ways of expressing yourself," I said.

"That is true," he said, locking eyes with me. "Do you write your own music?"

"I dabble," I said, "but I mostly play cover tunes for drunk crowds."

"That sounds like fun," said Dr. Terrific wryly.

For the first time that night, Haley looked up from her phone. "My dad is a great guitar player," she said.

"I'm sure he is," said Dr. Terrific. "Maybe Lauren and I will watch you play some night. Do you ever play college campuses? I teach at UNH."

I contemplated reaching across the table and ringing his pretentious neck. I could've made a noose for him with my thumb and index finger. "I'm not currently playing in a band, but my best friend is a drummer, and we're in the process of putting one together," I lied. While Alan and I have played in at least half a dozen bands together since high school, we currently aren't doing shit. I've been too busy gaining weight and watching *Law and Order.*

"You'll have to let us know," Dr. Terrific said, sipping his craft beer, some IPA that was probably hand-brewed by a cheese farmer in Vermont. "Who doesn't love a cover band?"

Haley stared at her water glass, tapping it with a clean fork. "You don't have to be a dick, Ryan," she said.

"Haley!" Lauren screamed.

Dr. Terrific laughed and folded his Smurf mitts in front of him. "It's okay, Lauren," he said. "Haley and I are having some growing pains. I'll admit that I'm not used to dealing with children."

"She's almost an adult," I said and looked at Haley.

With a smug grin and short laugh, Ryan sipped his beer then pursed his lips. "I'm not sure I would classify a fifteen-year-old as an adult."

"She is sixteen," I said, "and she's right. You are a dick."

"Please stop," Lauren said, shaking her head. "Can't everyone just be fucking civil?" Lauren seldom cursed.

In the silence that followed, amplified the rhythmic ticking from the grandfather clock in the hallway, another wave of itching exploded from my inner-thighs. I clamped my crotch and glanced across the table at my wife. "I should leave," I said.

"Dad, don't," Haley said. "I want you to stay." The comment caught all of us by surprise, and I choked up.

"I miss you, sweetie," I said to Haley.

Haley clutched her chest and fluttered her eyelashes. "And I miss you, father," she said in a strained British-accent. "And God bless us, everyone, except for Ryan because he's a dick."

Dr. Terrific tossed his napkin on the table and stood from his chair. "Maybe I should leave," he said, staring at me.

Crotch-aflame, I bit down on my cheeks and reached under the table to scratch. "I'm sorry, Ryan. Sit down. I'll get everyone a drink," I said, using this as an opportunity to slip into the bathroom and slather on another handful of Cortisone cream. "What's everyone having?"

"I'm sorry about my outburst as well," Dr. Terrific said. "I think we're all a little on edge and got off on the wrong foot. I'll have another IPA, Elliot. And thank you."

I nodded and turned to Lauren. "Wine is fine," she said.

"I'll have a vodka-cranberry with a lime," Haley said.

"Nice try," I said and dashed out of the dining room, up the staircase and into the bathroom again, where I did my deed and dashed back into the kitchen where I grabbed two bottles of beer—a Bud Light and an IPA—and the chardonnay I brought for Lauren. In the dining room, there was another thick silence when I entered. I placed the bottle of wine in front of Lauren and handed Dr. Terrific his bottle of beer.

Dr. Terrific snickered into a closed fist. "Is that Sutter Homes?" he asked. "Is this a dorm party? Are we going to Taco Bell afterwards?"

As the blood rushed to my cheeks, I dropped my head, feeling fat and itchy and ashamed. I glanced at Lauren, who poured herself a generous glass of Sutter Homes, cool and composed, and slugged the entire thing before pouring another. "Maybe you *should* leave," she said.

Dr. Terrific froze, his mouth hanging open and his diminutive index finger scratching the meticulously-groomed stubble on his cheek. "Lauren, come on. I was joking."

"I don't think you were," she said, staring at him over the top of her wine glass. "I happen to like Sutter Homes, and I've always liked Sutter Homes. I liked it in college, and I still like it today. Now get the fuck out of our house."

Haley bit her bottom lip as I shrugged at Dr. Terrific. I know this much after being married to the woman for so long: When Lauren gets going, it's best to step aside and let her go.

For a second time, Dr. Terrific stood up and spiked his napkin, squeezing his hands into dainty little fists. "I knew this was a bad idea. He clearly still has the hots for you, Lauren," he said. "You and Kip Winger deserve each other."

I folded my superior man hands on the table. For the first time in twenty-four hours, the itching had abated, and I didn't want to jinx anything. "It was really terrific meeting you," I said.

"Fuck you, fat ass," he said and left the room.

The three of us said nothing as the front door slammed and his Jeep started in the driveway. The headlights flashed in the dining room windows then disappeared. We all looked down at the tablecloth and waited for someone to speak.

Finally, Haley broke the silence. "That went better than I expected," she said.

We all burst into laughter.

The wall clock in Sadie's office ticks away as we wait. Lauren is half an hour late. Like a moron, I may have read far too much into the fact that I stayed at the house after Dr. Terrific left on Friday, and Lauren and I finished the Sutter Homes chardonnay then slept together, falling back into our old roles. I left the next morning after making a big breakfast of bacon, eggs and home fries for Lauren and Haley. I had an orange and black coffee. It was time to start my diet. But then Lauren didn't answer a single text that I sent her all weekend, leaving me perplexed.

Finally, she comes into the office without knocking and closes the door behind her. She's wearing a new overcoat, heels and a knee-length skirt, and holding a cup of Starbuck's coffee. "Sorry I'm late," she says. "I had to drop Haley off at school and caught some traffic."

Sadie smiles at Lauren. "Don't worry about it," she says. "Your ex-husband and I were enjoying some delightful conversation."

Something about the term "ex-husband" stabs me in my flabby gut. "Lauren, do you think you and I could talk in private first?"

Lauren stares me in the eyes, tilts her head to the side and frowns. "Ryan came back on Saturday afternoon and apologized," she says.

"Oh," I say.

There's a strange sensation in my groin as I process the words, a combination of itching and a stabbing pain. Stunned and sick, I turn away from Lauren and watch as Sadie takes the papers out of a manila envelope and places them on her desk in front of me. She extends a pen. "This will only take a second," she says. "Then we can all get on with our day."

RAIN

WHEN SHE SLIPS HER HEEL OFF under the table and runs her toe up the hem of your jeans, you whisper to her that you know a place. "It's called The Kozy 7," you say, "but it's a little seedy, and not so cozy."

"It sounds perfect," she says as the lights dim and a cover band of forty-something rockers start their second set by playing the piano solo to "Home Sweet Home" on an electric keyboard.

You pull into the parking lot, and there's a stretch of dilapidated motel rooms with chipped white paint and weak wooden awnings that an asthmatic breath could blow down. You can tell by the way she sighs that she didn't anticipate this type of seedy. A red "Vacancy" sign blinks in the window of the main office, and you cut the engine in your old sedan, realizing you're drunker than you thought you were when you left the bar. You fondle your wedding ring then check your wallet, stunned by your own stupidity. "I don't have enough cash," you tell her. "And I can't use my card. My wife checks our bank account every morning."

"So does my husband." She reaches into her purse and produces three twenties. "Will this be enough?"

You nod and take the cash and kiss her on the lips. "I have some Jameson in the trunk."

"Do they have an ice machine?"

"I'll check."

As you walk into the front office, there's a small dog—a Pomeranian, maybe—yipping at you. An old Vietnamese woman behind the front desk shushes him. Everything is tawdry, from the heavy red curtains covering the picture window to the black velvet painting of a hyacinth bush on the wall beside a digital clock that reads 11:12. And while you hand the clerk the cash and your driver's license, proof of who you are—a father of two teenage sons, a husband to a woman who hasn't slept with you in six months and vacillates between counseling and a divorce—you realize you're about to sleep with someone you hardly know, a colleague at the college where you teach as an adjunct, a woman as sad and frustrated and lonely as yourself. In the lobby of the main office, you quietly consent to all of this.

Back in the car, a key on a green plastic keychain dangles like an ugly Christmas ornament from your index finger, and you notice her head hung, her eyes focused on her phone.

You say, "I know it's not the Hilton—"

"Where are you telling your wife that you're staying tonight?"

"I don't know. What are you telling your husband?"

"I don't know."

The motel room reeks of stale cigarettes, bleached sheets and Febreze. A framed print of seashells hangs above the bed, dull and deaf. The mattress is high and covered in a stiff quilt with a gaudy floral design. A microwave rests atop a brown mini-fridge, and a flat screen television is mounted on the wall across from the bed. You sit on the edge of the mattress with the whiskey bottle between your legs.

"Is something wrong?" she asks, sitting beside you, kissing your cheek, reaching for the bottle.

You turn and kiss her mouth, her ear, the naked space below her neckline. She kneads your scalp and fakes a moan, such an actress. You place the bottle on the nightstand, shut off the light and, quick, you both slip out of your clothes. Now you're naked beneath the bleached sheets and the stiff quilt, in the dark.

"Are you, you know, fixed?" she asks. "Or do we need a condom?"

"I'm fixed," you say and remember the day you spent on the couch watching the Red Sox game with a bag of frozen peas and Vicodin, six months after your second son, Christopher, was born.

There's not much in the way of foreplay—some fumbling of hands seeking assurance, mouths seeking mouths, tongues seeking tongues. Then her tear drops on your nose, and your tear drops down the side of your face. They drop, and they drop.

THE UNICORN

AMY SQUEEZED HER HUSBAND'S HAND as the bartender placed a draft beer and a Chocolate Martini on the coasters in front of them. "Do you remember when the last time we were at a hotel bar was?" she asked Brad.

"At your sister's wedding in Portsmouth. A decade ago."

"I'm impressed," she said and smiled at the bartender, a handsome young man with dimples and a black bow tie. "Are you nervous?"

Brad sipped his beer. "I've been imagining all of the things that can go wrong."

"Me too."

Brad and Amy were overdressed for the Double Tree in Nashua on a Tuesday night. Amy wore a black dinner dress that felt tight on her hips and gold hoop earrings, and Brad had ironed a light blue button-down shirt and threw on a sports coat and new blue jeans. Neither of them knew what they were supposed to wear to an arrangement like this, so they collectively decided to look their best.

Amy took a sip of the martini then another longer gulp. "She was supposed to meet us at nine p.m.," she said. "It's ten past. Maybe we should call her."

"We'll give her another twenty minutes," Brad said, cracking his knuckles, a habit that never failed to make Amy cringe—one of the many small grievances, among some larger ones, that had landed them there.

A marriage counselor suggested that they try something out

of their comfort zone as an attempt to stoke the smoldering embers of a marriage that almost ended after their daughter's boyfriend—a young man they abhorred—slipped and hit his head on the concrete and drowned in their swimming pool. The young man's mother filed a wrongful death lawsuit that was still being litigated. Due to the tension created by the lawsuit, their daughter's nervous breakdown after the drowning, and the real possibility of losing the house, Brad and Amy had moved into separate bedrooms on separate floors in their home. Idle and alone at night, restless with a case of menopausal insomnia, Amy passed the hours of the night in the quiet house drinking wine and scrolling through social media. She ended up reconnecting with her college boyfriend, Ben, who had recently divorced his wife—Amy's former roommate—after eighteen years of marriage and three kids together. At first, their private messages were long laments about their spouses and some nostalgic revisions of their time together in college. But, gradually, the messages got more personal, then sexual, and then they began exchanging pictures in various stages of undress through text messages. Suspicious, Brad went through her phone one night after Amy had consumed two bottles of Pinot Grigio and passed out, and found a slew of lascivious messages and photos. The next morning, he checked into a motel, only to return home ten days later.

This whole night at The Double Tree, as Amy saw it, was about compensation, leveling the playing field after the things that Brad saw on her phone, and the things that he did not know.

Amy spotted the girl as soon as she walked through the glass doors into the hotel bar. Then Brad's phone buzzed. "That must be her," Amy said, pointing toward the entrance. "She's pretty."

Brads turned and waved as the couple inspected the young

woman squeezed into a strapless silver dress, wobbling a bit on her three-inch heels, and smiling as she approached. She had thin and delicate wrists with a bevy of silver bangles. She hid some of her natural beauty with an excess of eyeliner and lip-plumper, which appeared slightly more tawdry than sexy to Amy, making her look like a little girl who got into her mother's makeup bag. Up close, her face seemed rounder, as if she were still shedding baby fat. But Brad had assured Amy that the girl's age had been vetted by the escort agency—which Amy knew was a euphemism—where they found her profile on an online forum after searching for "unicorns."

"Are you sure she is twenty-one?" Amy whispered to Brad, still leery.

"Hopefully the bartender will card her," Brad said softly then stood and extended his hand. "You must be Nadia," he said.

"And you must be Bill and Cheryl," she said, shaking hands with Brad then Amy. "It's nice to meet you," the girl said without a trace of an accent. When Amy saw her name and profile, she assumed the girl would be Eastern European, possibly trafficked, which compounded her trepidation about this whole sordid arrangement.

"Can I buy you a drink?" Brad asked.

Nadia sat on the stool next to him, crossing her legs at the ankles, her dress hiking up her thighs. "A pineapple Truly," she said. "You have a room, right?"

Amy finished her first chocolate martini. "We're in Room 221. Why? Should we not be sitting together?"

"It doesn't matter," Nadia said. "I'll pretend I'm your niece."

"That sounds a little incestuous," Amy joked.

Nadia looked at her blankly.

"Nevermind."

Brad flagged down the bartender, who nodded at Nadia and grinned. "Hello, Nadia," he said and asked for her order without asking for an ID.

Amy nudged Brad. After the bartender brought Nadia her hard seltzer and a glass with ice, as well as Amy's second martini, Brad pushed back his stool so the three of them could chat, although the bar wasn't loud with only a handful of customers and some soft piano music piped through the ceiling.

"So how long have you been married?" Nadia said.

"Our twentieth-third anniversary is next week," Amy lied.

Nadia smiled with lipstick smeared on her front tooth. "Do you have kids?"

"We have a daughter," Amy said without making eye contact. "She is about your age." If anything could completely torpedo their plan, it would be a discussion about Ava, who still hadn't left the house, except for her therapy appointments, in almost eight months, and refused to work or take a college course. All day, she sat in her bedroom, catatonically scrolling through her phone. Amy had her doubts that her daughter would ever leave that bedroom again, or ever fully recover from the trauma of finding that boy face-down in the pool.

Brad finished his beer. "I'm going outside for a cigarette," he said and grabbed the pack of Marlboros from his shirt pocket. Brad only smoked cigarettes when he was nervous or drunk, preferring cigars.

"I'll join you," Nadia said, grabbing her purse from the bar top.

"I guess I'll save your seats," Amy joked, looking around the near-empty bar.

"You don't smoke?" Nadia asked.

"I quit when I was about your age," Amy said to Nadia.

Nadia flashed an inscrutable smile. "That's good. Smoking is bad for you."

Amy watched as her husband and their escort walked toward the entrance. She thought about slipping away and allowing Brad to have the night with the girl, alone. It only seemed fair, seeing Brad never found out about the night she met Ben at a bar in Boston. When she lifted her drink, which was almost empty again, the bartender was standing in front of her. "I can only serve you one more," he said. "We have a three martini limit."

As the booze coursed through her bloodstream, she shot him a flirty look, lashes fluttering. "We'll see about that."

Amy had not intended for things with Ben to go further than a few drinks that night, although she knew the possibility existed. She knew, ethically, that she was stepping out by showing up. They met at a crowded pub in the Back Bay and sat in a tall wooden booth. Ben's hair had thinned since college, when he wore it long and played the guitar in a band, and his face carried the bloat of a busy middle-aged man who drank too much beer and ate too much take-out, but he had maintained his boyish good looks, and Amy felt a sexual surge as the conversation flowed effortlessly, a continuation of their messaging, and they both consumed rounds of drinks. Then Amy's fingers reached across the table and grazed Ben's forearm, and the topics shifted into the spaces that they had been exploring with those pictures and private messages, and when the waitress informed them of the last call, their eyes met, and they knew.

In his hotel room, both were eager to show how they had refined their techniques since their days of messy intercourse as young adults. They devoted hours to each other's bodies, until daylight streamed across the foot of the queen-sized bed, catnapping briefly before dressing and parting in the hotel lobby with a hug and a quick peck on the lips.

When Amy returned home late-Sunday morning, Brad was lying on the couch in the living room, watching the Patriots' pre-game and barely acknowledging her. She went upstairs and showered then napped again. After waking up, she blocked Ben's number, unfriended him on social media, and swore to never speak to him again.

Later that day, she asked Brad if she could move back into their bedroom, and Brad agreed.

Nadia discarded her heels and strolled slowly around the hotel room, running her fingertips over the surface of the furniture as if she were checking for dust. A lamp on the nightstand lit the room. Amy and Brad were squeezed into a love seat in front of the windows with the heavy curtains drawn. Brad sipped from a Bud Light can he grabbed from the mini-bar. Tipsy from the three martinis, Amy had poured a glass of tap water into a plastic cup that she found next to the coffee machine.

"So how does this work?" Amy asked the girl.

Nadia reached into her purse and took out a vape. "I'm yours for the night," she said. "I will do as little or as much as you'd like with either of you, only no anal stuff." Nadia then unzipped the back of her dress and slipped out of it with a graceful, theatrical half-step. She wore black panties and a matching strapless bra, which she removed before falling onto her back on the mattress.

Brad folded his hands over his lap. "Should we get undressed?" he asked.

Nadia hit on the vape pen then said, "You can do whatever you'd like, but don't you want to play with each other first?"

Brad patted Amy's thigh, like he had finished a pep talk, and stood up from the love seat. Amy watched as he took off the dress shirt and jeans and sat back down beside her in his boxer briefs, his erection tenting outward. Amy closed her eyes and dropped the straps on her dress as Brad cupped her breast, squeezing a bit too hard, and pressed his mouth against hers. His lips were cold and stiff, as if he had just come up from cool water.

As he worked his tongue in her mouth, Amy could not stop thinking about the young girl on the bed, watching them with her vape pen, bored. She could not shake the fact that the girl reminded her of her own daughter, who was certainly sitting in her bedroom, scrolling through her phone.

"Let's go to the bed," Amy whispered into her husband's ear.

Brad made a feral noise of consent and stood again. Amy watched as her husband—led by his sad hard-on—made the short walk onto the bed where Nadia held out her hand. "Are you coming, Cheryl?"

Amy looked at them lying on the bed, Brad kissing Nadia's breasts. "I need to use the bathroom first," Amy said, pulling up the straps on her dress and walking past the bed and down the narrow hall toward the bathroom on her left. But instead of turning into the bathroom, she quietly opened the door to the room and slipped out into the well-lit hallway and turned right toward the elevator, which she rode to the hotel lobby. From the lobby, she walked outside and stood in the fresh night air under the car port. To her left, the bartender was sitting on a bench, smoking a cigarette. He waved, and Amy waved back.

"I thought you went upstairs," the bartender said, knowing.

"I did."

"Where is your husband?"

"Upstairs," she said. "Can I bum one of those?"

The bartender reached into his shirt pocket then handed her a lighter and a pack of American Spirits. "I thought I heard you say that you didn't smoke," he said.

"I used to smoke," said Amy, lighting a cigarette, "but I quit."

A Long Way from New Hampshire

A COUPLE OF CREEPS come out of the gas station carrying six packs of beer and staring long and hard at my chest. I'm standing beside the propane tanks, waiting for my new boyfriend Aaron and his cousin to return from wherever they went to score weed. Aaron said the weed was a sure thing, but we're in Brownsville, Tennessee, a long way from New Hampshire, and I have no idea where he went.

I shiver thinking about these creeps. They look like the types of dangerous rednecks who could have their way with a girl, cut her throat then dump her body like a sack of broken heels somewhere in the hills. Before my mom got sick, she used to say to me, "Jenny, if you're going to dress like that, with hardly any clothes, then men are going to look at you and get some ideas. It's not right, but it's the truth."

Maybe she was right: the looks in these creeps' eyes leave nothing to my imagination. I know what they're thinking. I know those ideas. But Mom is more than a thousand miles away right now, dying, and I'm here to fend for myself. I'm hoping the creeps will get a good look and keep walking right past me, but I'm not so lucky. They stop about six feet in front of me, scratching the stubble on their cheeks and smiling at me. The taller of the two creeps, who has a lazy eye that makes him even creepier, holds out a can of beer. "Want one?"

"No thanks."

"Do you need a ride somewhere, sweetie, or are you just

prettying up these here propane tanks?" says the tall creep then he winks at me. "I'm Jake, and this here is Keith, but we call him Digger. I got some weed in the truck if your sweet ass is interested in strapping on a buzz with us."

"My boyfriend will be here any minute," I say and look down at my phone to keep from making eye contact.

"He ain't here now," Jake says then rubs his you-know-what. "We can drive around a little, burn one and have you back before he gets here. We'll have you back in ten minutes. However long it takes."

"No thanks." My skin is prickling. Not again, I think. I want to scream, but I can't get enough air in my lungs. Not again.

"I'm not sure where you're from, sugar tits, but around here if you hang out in front of stores, guys are going to think you're offering it."

The other guy, the one they call Digger, spits tobacco juice in the dirt. "Fucking tease."

Then they turn and walk slowly back to their pick-up truck, glancing over their shoulders as my heart hammers in my chest. They start the truck, rev the engine and peel out of the dirt lot. Then, while driving past me, Digger sticks his head out the passenger side window. "Fucking whore!"

Dark clouds drift across the sky and a breeze whips through my hair, which I recently dyed black. A raindrop falls on my cheek, and another one on my forearm, and then one on my nose. I wonder when, or if, Aaron is coming back. I wonder whether I should go inside the store and wait. I wonder what my mom would say if I bought a bus ticket and showed up at the house, dressed like this, and said, "Mom, I want to come home."

FISHBONE

MY SPONSOR RICK WAS WORRIED. My wife and I had sold the house, and I was meeting her for dinner at a seafood restaurant on the coast in Portsmouth. I told Rick the dinner was about closure for me, closing on the house but also about trying to move past the hurt and forgive her for sleeping with another man while accepting my own fault in the matter.

"You've only been sober four months, Mark," Rick said over the phone as I choked down a cigarette, resting on my crutches outside the entrance to The Lobster's Claw, a place Lisa and I would frequent when we were dating in college. I suppose you could call it *our* place. "At this point," he said, "you should try to avoid situations that could trigger a relapse, and meeting your ex at a bar sounds like one of those situations."

"I'll order a Diet Coke and call you if I get into trouble," I said, watching my four-legged shadow on the sidewalk. I still didn't have the heart, or the courage, to tell him that I had started drinking again the night before my alleged third month of sobriety, and now I was drinking in my apartment every night after coming home from the AA meetings.

Rick said, "First things first."

I turned to my left and saw Lisa walking toward the restaurant, her heels clicking on the concrete. I dropped the lit cigarette and crushed it with my sandal on the foot without the cast. "I have to go, Rick. I'll call you later," I said and tucked my phone into the pocket of my cargo shorts.

After five months without seeing Lisa, the sight of her socked me. Her long hair was stacked loosely on top of her head, her white neck gleaming in the summer evening light. She wore a short paisley sundress with heels. I couldn't tell if she had lost weight, gained some, or somehow redistributed it in the right places. The thought that this other man, her editor, was climbing into bed—our old bed, I assumed—with her each night was a second punch, this time below the belt.

"You look great," I said.

"It's good to see you, Mark," Lisa said and smiled, her eyes cast downward like she was visiting a sick friend at the hospital. "How is the leg?" She grimaced.

"It's healing."

"Did you get a reservation?"

"It's at seven," I said and grabbed my phone and checked the time. "We have a few minutes."

"Do you want to go in and have a…" She paused and placed her hand over her mouth, like she was trying to stuff the words back in it. We'd been talking on the phone and sending e-mails, mostly about selling the house, but I had also lied to her about my alleged sobriety in a desperate attempt to impress her. I wanted Lisa to see me as a new man, a man capable of making good, sound decisions. "I'm sorry," she said. "Old habit."

"It's all right," I said. An ocean breeze skipped off the water and cooled my cheeks. "I can order a soda."

"How long has it been?"

"Four months and two weeks." I took my four month chip from my pocket to show her then performed my old sleight of hand trick, making it disappear.

"I see you're still doing the trick," she said and grazed my arm with her fingernails. "How do you feel?"

"Like a new man, except for the busted ankle." To buy time, I lit another cigarette and offered her the open pack.

"When did you start smoking?" She asked and took one from my pack.

"I swapped out vices."

"I suppose it's for the best."

The Friday night crowd at the bar on the back deck rumbled like a chest cough. The band wouldn't start until later, but the drinkers dedicated to landing bar stools had showed up early and staked out their ground.

Lisa glanced over her shoulder before she lit the cigarette then inhaled it deeply and exhaled loudly. "I told Ron that I quit," she said. His name, coming from her mouth, seemed vulgar, like a cuss.

"Don't worry," I said. "I won't tell him."

Rick would say that everything happens for a reason. He would say there's a divine order to the chain of events in our lives, good and bad, and the imperceptible hand of a higher power is constantly moving them into place. Rick believes that we can choose whether or not to listen when our higher power speaks to us or, as he would say, we can willfully play the fool. While I could never fully get my head around the whole higher power concept, even I have to admit, some things happen that defy my belief that everything is thrown in the air and lands in random patterns, and we can choose to either assign meaning to these patterns, or not. In other words, Rick would say that the table where you sit at a restaurant is not pure chance, but part of some divine plan that you can't possibly understand. In this case, maybe he was right.

Lisa and I were seated at a table in the back corner of the dining room by a window looking out on the deck and the band setting up. Beyond the deck, the Atlantic stretched until it melded with the horizon, its slow surf slapping against the thick wooden posts supporting the back deck, finally stopping on a small piece of private shoreline. As the unpleasant discussions about the impending sale of the house, our final tie to each other, and our impending divorce stuck in our throats like fishbones, we watched the tide, inhaled the salty air from the open window, and waited for someone to take our drink orders.

A waitress, college-aged with a heart-shaped face, came to the table with a pad in her hand, bouncing on her toes. "Can I get you guys something to drink?"

I knew without looking that Lisa was rolling her eyes, peeved that the waitress used the term "guys" when speaking to a female. But the waitress's question also startled me. Any previous time that I had dined at The Lobster's Claw, my standard response was to order a Sam Adams on tap and sidecar of Jameson. Then I remembered my sober story and paused.

"I'll have a Chardonnay." Lisa nervously tucked a stray strand of hair behind her ear, melting me. "If that's all right with you?"

I waved my hand. No sweat. Then the waitress turned to me. I gazed out at the water, the deck, and the drinkers—my people—laughing and sipping their drinks. "I'll have a Diet Coke."

"I'll be right back with those," the waitress said and scampered away into the seafood-scented dining room full of nautical paraphernalia—an old chipped captain's wheel mounted on the wall with a banged-up orange buoy and black and white photographs of bearded fishermen standing on the bows of ships, smoking pipes with the docks in the background.

"She's cute," Lisa said after the waitress was out of earshot. "Are you dating anyone?"

My mouth opened then closed. "My sponsor suggested I stay away from new relationships for the first year of sobriety," I told her, instead of the truth, which was that I had a brief fling with a woman in the program that ended badly, and since then, I had been sleeping with a woman who I met at a bar one night, who was going through her own divorce, and would be out the door as soon as we finished having sex to relieve the babysitter who she couldn't really afford.

"That makes sense," Lisa said. "So how is Gary?" Gary was a parrot, and one of the few things I was allowed to take when I moved out of the house.

"Still chatting up a storm," I said.

"That's good to hear," Lisa said as she stared at the ocean.

I tapped on my water glass. "It's really good to see you, Lisa. There are so many things that I've wanted to say to you."

"So say them."

"I wish I could have a fucking drink."

Lisa bristled. "Maybe this wasn't a good idea," she said. "I didn't mean to put you in a bad spot, Mark. I just thought that this would all be easier, better, if we could still be friends and settle all of this peacefully."

"Right. Friends. We can be friends," I said. "That's good. That's fine. I'm cool with being friends."

At the table next to us, an old couple was picking at a plate of calamari and not speaking. They stared down at the food like they had used up all their dinner conversations decades ago and there were no words left to share. The only noise they had left was the dull scraping of their utensils on the plates. At that moment, while watching the old couple, I wanted Lisa with a yearning that bordered on pathological. I was kicking myself for all of those nights that I could've had her and didn't; for all of those nights that she'd made her body available to me, and I chose pills and booze instead; for all of those nights when I came to bed, blasted, and rejected her advances in favor of a dreamless sleep. With my insane jealousy and my paranoia that she was cheating on me before she did, as well as my manic mood crashes, it wasn't surprising she looked elsewhere for attention. Like my father before me, I was a fucking asshole in my marriage. Since moving out of our house, I'd spent many nights, alone and anguished, realizing that maybe I forced her into the bed of another man who would notice her, appreciate her.

I swallowed hard and worked up the courage to say what I had come there to say. "I miss you," I said. "I feel like I don't know you anymore, and it's killing me."

Lisa squeezed her eyes shut. "I'm glad you're getting better."

The waitress came back with our drinks and placed them on beer coasters. "Would you like to order an appetizer, or do you need more time to look at the menu?"

"We'll have the crab cakes," we said at the same time.

The waitress smiled. "That's so cute. How long have you guys been together?"

Lisa picked up her wine and took a careful sip, her lipstick staining the rim of the glass. "We're just friends," she said.

I died a little.

With their appetizer plates cleared, the old couple sucked iceless water through clear straws, frowning and looking in opposite directions. They were one of those couples who had begun to resemble one another, the type who, as they grow old, begin to look more like siblings, not spouses. The woman had short, gray hair with a mannish cut and thin rigid lips. The skin on her face, bullied by gravity, was snagged into a perpetual scowl. The man had a similar haircut, although his hair was clipped slightly shorter, with the same droopy face and tight mouth—as if both of them had sealed any affection for each other deep in the catacombs of their coldness. They sat across from each other like they were dining alone, sulking in silence.

"There's something else I need to tell you," I said and reached across the table for Lisa's hand. She let me hold it for a moment before gently pulling it away.

"What is it?"

I wanted—and maybe I intended—to tell her everything about how I hated my crappy one-bedroom apartment in a seedy section of Manchester; how I spent three miserable days in county jail after my last DUI and soundlessly cried in my cell each night; how I couldn't sleep when I was sober, imagining her in bed with her editor, imagining him admiring the way she bites down lightly on her bottom lip and moans softly before she's about to orgasm. I wanted to tell her how sometimes I faked getting off with the woman I met at the bar so we could stop, how the whole thing had nothing to do with getting off, and I just wanted to be touched by a woman. I wanted to tell her that I didn't want to sell the house that we bought together and sever that last frayed tie. I wanted to stop the act and tell Lisa the truth that I wasn't sober, and I wasn't happy, and I wasn't ready to let her go. But I didn't. Instead, I grabbed a napkin on the table and scrunched it into a ball. "I'm sorry."

"You have nothing to be sorry about," Lisa said, frowning.

"But I do," I said. "It's my fault we're selling the house. All of this is my fault. If I wasn't so selfish and wasted all the time, you never would've done what you did. I drove you to it, and now I want to put this in reverse and go back and make it better. Can't we try to make it better?" My voice cracked.

The sun was setting on the horizon, and a blinding pool of orange light bounced off the surface of the water. Then Lisa reached over and placed her hand, like a lacey shroud, on top of my balled fist. She said, "I'm sorry, too. It's my fault, too. I wasn't nice to you."

As I squinted to see her face, the bombast of light reflecting off the water obscured her, and all I saw was the silhouette of the woman who was my wife. "Do you love him?" I asked.

"Mark, don't." She pulled back her hand, and before I could respond, a plate of crab cakes was placed between us. Lisa sighed with relief and reached for her fork, and I reached for my beer. But it wasn't there. I grabbed my crutches from the floor and hoisted myself up from the table.

"I have to use the bathroom," I said then hobbled out of the dining room toward the hostess station at the entrance of the restaurant where you could turn right for the restrooms or left onto the deck and the bar. I turned left.

With the jukebox cranking in the corner and the band running a sound check on the deck, I gimped up to the bar and rested on my crutches beside two college-aged guys on stools. I flagged down the bartender, a stout man around my age who had been working at the bar since Lisa and I first started going there. After filling a beer and placing it on a waitress's tray, he glanced at me.

"What can I get you, buddy?"

I allowed my shoulders to relax. "I'll have a shot of Cuervo," I said.

"You look familiar," said the bartender, reaching behind him for the bottle. "You used to come here. I remember your face."

"When I was younger, yes."

"You used to come in with this really gorgeous woman, right?"

I nodded. "I married her."

The bartender pursed his lips and placed the shot in front of me. "Lucky guy," he said.

"I sure am." I reached into my pocket and pulled out a ten dollar bill and placed it on the bar top. I then picked up the shot and tossed it back. When I put down the glass, there was a sip of the clear liquor left, settled in the bottom of the glass. So I finished it then hobbled out, grabbing two peppermints from the hostess's station.

When I sat down, Lisa was eating a crab cake. "Are you all right?"

"I went out for a cigarette," I said and sipped my Diet Coke.

"Right," she said. "You seem to be feeling better."

I wanted a second drink but scooped a crab cake onto my plate instead. "I'm fine," I said. "Everything is great."

Lisa and I ordered our entrees, a fried clam plate and a fried scallop dinner, which we would share when we were together, but I doubted there would be any communal eating when the food arrived. She ordered a second glass of wine. On the deck, the band was about to start, and Lisa picked at her clams with her fork.

"I wish the couple buying the house gave us our asking price," she said without looking up from the plate. "But it's enough to break even."

"Where are you going to live?" I asked. Lisa had told me that she was still living in the house, alone, but I knew that her boyfriend stayed there quite a bit, and probably had a toothbrush.

"I'm going to live with Ron until I find my own place," said Lisa.

"I guess it's pretty serious."

"I guess." We both stared out at the ocean and the small waves finishing the long trek to the shore. "Our neighbor, Darla, she isn't doing well."

"I'm sorry to hear that."

"There is a hospice nurse who goes there every day. I don't think she has a lot of time left. And her husband told me that their teenage daughter ran away. It's so sad. She's so young."

"Which one?"

"Both."

"Do you remember the time you flashed Wayne and his friends when I was drinking with them in the driveway?"

Lisa laughed. "I was so pissed off at you."

"We moved past it."

"Things were different," Lisa said with her head turned to the window and her hand pressed lightly to her throat. We watched the last of the daylight strain from the sky as the floodlights on the deck switched on.

A clamor came from the old couple's table. A plate smashed, and a chair overturned. The old man stood up and, like a boxer stunned by a punch, he started to stagger backwards. He bumped into Lisa's chair, changed course, and fell onto his table. The old woman watched wide-eyed, mouthing his name: "Richard." Then she said it a second time, soft and careful as the old man's hands went to his throat and his face had turned a purplish-blue. His wife's mouth opened again and, finally, the scream erupted. "Richard!"

Everyone in the dining room had turned toward the commotion and watched with horror as the old man rolled from the table and fell to the ground. A waiter and a cook ran from the kitchen and tried to lift him to his feet.

Lisa reached across the table and grabbed my hand. "What's wrong with him, Mark?"

I shrugged, unable to speak.

The old woman held her head in her hands, screaming her husband's name, as the cook, a large guy with a handlebar mustache and a Harley Davidson doo-rag, propped up the old guy and stood behind him with his fist jammed below his ribcage, thrusting inward. The old man hung like a wet leaf from his arms.

"Mark, is he dead?" Lisa asked, her voice quivering.

I said nothing. The old man's wife was petting her husband's hair, screaming his name, hysterical. That's when I caught a glimpse of the old man's face. His eyes were wide, his mouth open, his last breath as distant as the daylight the ocean had just swallowed. I knew the answer to Lisa's question but the words were stuck in my throat. I nodded.

I handed Lisa another cigarette as she walked and I hobbled under the streetlights to her car, which was parked in front of Murphy's Pub, an Irish bar where we used to go in the winters when The Lobster's Claw was closed.

We stood side-by-side, like strangers at a bus stop. "Do you need a ride back to Manchester?" she asked.

"I have a motel room," I said and looked at the heavy wooden door, the entrance to the bar. "Can I ask you something personal?"

"Only if I don't have to answer," she said.

"Does your boyfriend know you're here? With me?"

Lisa bit down on her bottom lip, killing me. "I told him I was having dinner with my girlfriends. Can I ask you something personal?"

"Only if I don't have to answer."

"Are you really sober?"

We locked eyes, and I lifted my hand to her cheek, my wife, while resting my weight on the crutches. "Can I buy you a drink?" I asked her.

"I knew it," she said. "You went to the bar outside and ordered a drink before dinner. Did you order another one after the paramedics arrived? When you said you had to use the bathroom again?"

I smiled sheepishly. "Will you have a drink with me?"

Lisa seemed to consider my offer. She held up her index finger. "One drink," she said and turned toward the entrance to the bar. "But that's it."

"I'll meet you inside," I said and reached into my pocket and grabbed my phone and the four-month chip. "I have to make a call."

He answered right away. "How did it go?"

"Listen, Rick," I said, flipping the chip in the air then letting it fall to the ground. "There's something I need to tell you."

PUBLICATION NOTES

Many thanks to the editors of the following publications—many of which are now obsolete—where these stories originally appeared: *Bananafish*, *The Coe Review*, *Controlled Burn*, *Drunk Monkeys*, *Falling Star Magazine*, *Flash Fiction Magazine*, *Freight Stories*, *Full of Crow*, *The Hawaii Review*, *Illinois English Bulletin*, *Night Train*, *Sententia*, *Storyglossia*, *Trailer Park Quarterly* and *Wilderness House Literary Review*.

"Vandals" was the winner of 2013 Luminaire Award for Prose, and "Fishbone" was a finalist for The Norman Mailer Award in 2011.

Some of these pieces were originally published—some in different forms—in my book *Almost Christmas* (Redneck Press, 2017).

Nathan Graziano lives in Manchester, New Hampshire, with his wife and a pug named Buster. This is his eleventh book. For more information, visit his website: www.nathangraziano.com

MORE ROADSIDE PRESS TITLES

By Plane, Train or Coincidence
Michele McDannold

Prying
Jack Micheline, Charles
Bukowski and Catfish
McDaris

*Wolf Whistles Behind the
Dumpster*
Dan Provost

*Busking Blues: Recollections of a
Chicago Street Musician
and Squatter*
Westley Heine

Unknowable Things
Kerry Trautman

How to Play House
Heather Dorn

Kiss the Heathens
Ryan Quinn Flanagan

St. James Infirmary
Steven Meloan

Street Corner Spirits
Westley Heine

*A Room Above
a Convenience Store*
William Taylor Jr.

Resurrection Song
George Wallace

*Nothing and Too Much
to Talk About*
Nancy Patrice Davenport

*Bar Guide for the
Seriously Deranged*
Alan Catlin

Born on Good Friday
Nathan Graziano

Under Normal Conditions
Karl Koweski

The Dead and the Desperate
Dan Denton

Clown Gravy
Misti Rainwater-Lites

Walking Away
Michael D. Grover

All in a Pretty Little Row
Dan Provost

*These Are the People in
Your Neighbourhood*
Jordan Trethewey

*They Said I Wasn't
College Material*
Scot Young

Radio Water
Francine Witte

And Blackberries Grew Wild
Susan Mickelberry

Licorice Heart
Miles Budimir

Disposable Darlings
Todd Cirillo

MORE ROADSIDE PRESS TITLES

Full Moon Midnight
Belinda Subraman

Innocent Postcards
John Pietaro

Cistern Latitudes
James Duncan

*Another Saturday Night
in Jukebox Hell*
Alan Catlin

Abandoned By All Things
Karl Koweski

Ain't These Sorrows Sweet?
Lauren Scharhag

*Gregory Corso:
Ten Times a Poet*
Edited by Leon Horton

*She Throws Herself Forward
to Stop the Fall*
Dave Newman

*We Don't Get to
Write the Ending*
Aleathia Drehmer

*These Many Cold
Winters of the Heart*
Ryan Quinn Flanagan

*Things You Never
Knew Existed*
Josh Olsen

Maze
Jennifer Juneau

Green Roses Bloom for Icarus
Hiromi Yoshida

Let the Scaffolds Fall
Shaun Rouser

Apocalypsing
Jason Anderson

Failing to Fall
James Griffin

Last Bacchanale
George Wallace

Thrift Store Jackets
Karl Koweski

Night Bird Flying
Danny Shot

*All Skate: True Stories
from Middle Life*
Lori Jakiela

*Cloud Watching
in the Inferno*
Westley Heine

Current Disasters
Jen McConnell

*Better Than The
Best American Poetry*
Dave Newman

Little Graveyards
Aleathia Drehmer

The Screw City Poems
Richard Vargas

MORE ROADSIDE PRESS TITLES

and all of us drinking the blood
of our enemies
John Sweet

This Is Where We Are
Nicholas Claro

Perseverance: The Making
of a Musician
Steven Grey

with her hair on fire
Christy Prahl

Fatherless Children
Michael D. Grover

The People Are Like
Wolves to Me
William Taylor Jr.